Granny Prue's Bucket List

PATRINA McKENNA

This book is a work of fiction. Names, characters, places, and incidents either are products of the author's imagination or are used fictitiously. Any resemblance to actual persons, living or dead, events, or locales is entirely coincidental.

Publisher: Patrina McKenna

patrina.mckenna@outlook.com

ISBN-13: 978-0-9932624-8-7

Also by Patrina McKenna

Feel good fantasy for the whole family!

GIANT Gemstones
A Galaxy of Gemstones
The Gemstone Dynasty
Enrico's Journey
Summer Camp at Tadgers Blaney Manor

Romantic comedy with a twist!

Truelove Hills
Truelove Hills – Mystery at Pebble Cove
Truelove Hills – The Matchmaker
Granny Prue's Bucket List

DEDICATION

For my family and friends

1

BACK TO REALITY

Lilly unlocked the door of her second-floor apartment. The armful of mail that had been accumulating in her post-box downstairs for the last month met with a thud on the hall floor. Lilly dropped her overnight bag on top of the leaflets, magazines, and letters before pushing the door shut behind her. That was it! Another failed relationship. Why, oh why, couldn't a twenty-six-year-old, single woman find love? It wasn't too much to ask, was it?

A quick look in the fridge turned her stomach. The excitement of spending time with her latest online admirer hadn't allowed for throwing milk away, or any perishables that were now covered in a furry green mould. How was she to know the weekend would turn into a month?

Lilly sighed as she reached for her phone charger. It was time to face reality. She'd not charged her phone for the last two weeks; the commiseration messages were becoming unbearable. She'd only lost her job, for goodness sake. No-one had died. It was time to get a grip now though and get her CV out there. Executive Assistants were in big demand in London. OK, the town of Tillingtree was a two-hour each way commute to London – maybe she'd find something closer to home if she was prepared to take a huge salary drop from her previous cushy role that she'd never appreciated until it was gone.

The pile of post needed dealing with next. Why was Lilly's mother writing to her? They were rarely in contact since Eloise had moved to Spain with her latest toy boy. The message inside the envelope was written in capital letters: PHONE ME. Typical of her mother, no "love from" or even a kiss. Lilly would phone her mother when it suited her, not when she was ordered to.

After shoving her washing into the machine and disinfecting her fridge, Lilly's phone rang.

'Lilly Prudance Lavender, you are the most difficult person in the world to get hold of. Where have you been? No, don't tell me. I don't want to know the sordid details. All I need is for you to get down here by lunchtime tomorrow.'

Lilly raised her eyes to the ceiling. 'Hello, Mother. Before you complain, I won't be getting down to Spain tomorrow, or at any time soon. You may remember that I need to find a job, and I am going to focus all my energy on that starting from now.'

'I don't mean Spain, Lilly. You need to get down to Cornwall. Granny Prue has died, and her funeral is at two o'clock tomorrow in that little church she always made us go to on Sundays when we spent all those wet and miserable summer holidays at hers when your father was alive. I arrived here this morning and have booked a room at the Hilton International, eight miles away. There are plenty of guest houses nearer to Starminster if you choose to stay overnight tomorrow. They will be more in your price range.'

*

It was dark when Lilly climbed into her car before dawn. She had a six-hour drive ahead. A long time alone, in which to reflect. How old would Granny Prue have been? She'd had her eightieth birthday some time ago. Lilly always received a letter from her Granny each birthday and Christmas. The last she'd heard was that she was very happy in her nursing home and that her carers regularly wheeled her onto the beach so that she could watch the children playing and look out to sea.

Those wet holidays in Cornwall weren't miserable for Lilly. She'd enjoyed spending time with her Granny. She'd had the undivided attention of her father too and the only downside of the holiday could be accredited to her mother's desire not to be there. Granny Prue made the most amazing light and fluffy scones and her jars of homemade jam always came back with the family to London. Granny knew how many jars they would need until their next annual visit.

Lilly's father was always happiest when they were in Cornwall, but Eloise's job as editor of a fashion magazine meant they needed to live in the City when Lilly was growing up. After her father died when she was fourteen, the visits to Granny Prue ceased. By the time Lilly was eighteen, her mother had suggested she "flee the nest". Eloise had been more than happy to fund the purchase of a new apartment for her only daughter. Of course, she had an ulterior motive, Lilly's exit from the London house paved the way for Eloise's latest love interest to move in.

With just one short stop at the Motorway Services for coffee and no delays on the roads, Lilly was relieved to see the sign for "Starminster". She drove along the seafront and parked in the Pay & Display car park. Her body felt stiff from sitting down for so long on the drive down, so Lilly stretched her arms above her head and breathed in the sea air. She wondered if the quaint tea room was still open. It was lunchtime now, and with just a coffee mid-morning, Lilly was hungry. Come to think of it; she'd only eaten a packet of biscuits last night after the call from her mother. She really should eat better.

Memories flooded back as Lilly walked along the promenade: Mrs Craddock's Tea Room was still there, along with Flora's Fish & Chip Shop, Alfie's Pasties & Pies, and the Blue Seagull public house. The smell of freshly cooked fish and chips competed with the aroma of traditional Cornish pasties – pure heaven. Lilly wandered into Alfie's shop. 'A traditional pasty please and a Diet Coke.'

Alfie looked over his glasses. 'Why it's Prue's granddaughter, isn't it? We've not seen you down here for many a year. Prue always gave us updates, though. We hear you're quite the businesswoman now, some sort of Executive. I expect you're down for the old girl's funeral. It should be a good do. Prue planned it herself.'

Lilly swallowed hard and wiped her eyes. She managed to smile at Alfie before paying for her lunch and wandering over the road to sit on the sea wall. A crushing feeling of guilt washed over her. She hadn't seen Granny Prue since her father's funeral over twelve years ago. She had written whenever there was any exciting news to divulge, but that hadn't been often.

'Excuse me, Miss, but you can't sit there. We're

closing the promenade from one o'clock today.'

Lilly looked up to witness two police officers standing before her. 'I'm sorry, I didn't know. I'll be on my way.'

After dropping her half-eaten pasty and empty can of drink into the nearest bin, Lilly looked at her watch. It was twelve-forty-five – those police officers were keen. Lilly looked up at the small church on the hill. She had over an hour to spare, so she decided to go for a stroll around the village.

'Hello, Lilly. We've been expecting you. Prue said you wouldn't miss her funeral.' Another pang of guilt encompassed her as she stood face to face with Mrs Carmichael, her Granny's next-door neighbour.

'Hello, Mrs Carmichael. How lovely to see you. Do you still live at Moonbeam Mews?'

'I moved from there a long time ago, dear. Those properties are falling down. I had no electricity for six months before I finally decided it was time to move on. I have a nice little apartment now with all mod cons. I've managed to stay out of a nursing home for now – I'm a bit younger than Prue was.'

'Did you remain friends with Granny, even when she was in the nursing home?'

'Oh, yes, dear. I visited her regularly, still the same

piercing violet eyes and mischievous personality until the day she died.'

Lilly stifled a sob. 'How did she die, Mrs Carmichael? Was it due to old age?'

'Oh, no, dear. Prue was reading one of her books to the residents at the home. She was laughing so much her false teeth became dislodged and choked her. Still, dying laughing was a fitting way for her to go. I bet she's laughing up there now.'

'Did my Granny write books, Mrs Carmichael? I never knew.'

'Oh, Lilly, dear, there will be lots of things you don't know about your grandmother. How can you know everything when someone's lived for over eighty years? Prue was a crafty one; I'll give that to her. We'd best keep an eye on the time. It's one-thirty now. May I hold your arm on the climb up the hill? We can't be late for Prue's funeral.'

2

A WAKE TO REMEMBER

Reverend Hartley stood outside the church, chatting to the gathered crowd. 'As it's such a lovely spring day, I'll leave the church door open so that everyone can hear the service. St Mary's only has seating capacity for sixty-four. Please come inside now and take your seats, for those that are able. Prudance wishes to make a grand entrance.'

Lilly and Mrs Carmichael entered the church and sat down next to Eloise, who was already seated in the front pew. She lifted her black veil before speaking. 'You made it then. I have no idea where all these people have come from. I was advised by the nursing home that your grandmother had the arrangements in hand for her funeral. I can only presume she's booked a buffet somewhere, hence the scavengers that have turned up.'

By two o'clock the congregation had fallen silent in anticipation of Prue's arrival. You could hear a pin drop inside and outside the church for the next ten minutes. The crunching of tyres on the gravel driveway alerted the mourners to the arrival of the hearse. Reverend Hartley walked down the aisle and took his position at the front before announcing: 'Please be upstanding, everyone.'

The organist shifted uneasily on her stool and stared at the sheet music which she didn't need to read. This was a piece that she knew off by heart. After taking a deep breath, she began to play.

Lilly shot a look at her mother before whispering. 'It's "Here Comes the Bride", they've got the wrong music.' Eloise looked over her shoulder to see a white coffin being carried down the aisle with a bouquet of blue irises on top.

Reverend Hartley smiled at the sea of stunned faces. 'We all knew Prudance, otherwise we wouldn't be here today. It shouldn't be surprising that she didn't want to leave this earth before completing her bucket list. There was always one thing that escaped her, and that was walking down the aisle to the Wedding March. Prudance knew she had to adjust her target near to the end of her life, and she changed that particular item to being "carried down the aisle by four eligible bachelors". I am pleased that we were able to honour her final wish today.'

Eloise smirked and whispered to Lilly, 'Eligible for what? She's dead.' Mrs Carmichael started the clapping which reverberated both inside and outside the church. Tears flowed and smiles preceded laughter. Prue would have loved the warm embrace in which her memory was becoming immortalised.

Reverend Hartley proceeded to conduct an uplifting service, and by three o'clock, the white coffin was being lowered into the ground under a magnolia tree in St Mary's churchyard. Lilly turned to her mother. 'It's not Granny in that coffin, is it? It's just her old body. Granny's looking down on us, isn't she? Her soul must be somewhere else.'

Eloise spoke from beneath her veil. 'If that's what you would like to think! Well, I've done my bit to represent your father. I'll not be staying around for any curled-up cucumber sandwiches. My driver's waiting for me. Make sure to keep in touch and try not to go missing again for weeks on end.' Eloise blew a kiss to Lilly then turned around and tottered off.

Mrs Carmichael threaded an arm through Lilly's. 'Your Granny will never leave us. Her spirit is all around. She'll be smiling down on you, my dear. You were her only grandchild. She only ever wanted the best for you.'

Lilly stifled a sob. 'I never knew Granny Prue hadn't been married. Did my grandfather die or run off? No-one's ever mentioned it, and I didn't like to ask. I suppose I presumed he'd died.'

Mrs Carmichael lowered her eyes. 'Oh, it was a long time ago, dear, and a very sad tale. Prue didn't speak about it much, except to say that your grandfather promised to meet her at Moonbeam Mews. They were madly in love at the time, but he never turned up. I'm sure she moved into Moonbeam Mews just in case he turned up one day, but he never did.'

The mourners dispersed in the direction of the seafront. Mrs Carmichael patted Lilly's hand and advised that she was off for her afternoon nap – Lilly felt lost. It was nearly three-thirty, if she got on the road again before four o'clock, and didn't stop on the way, she should be home by ten. Her head thumped, and her shoulders sagged as she trudged down the hill towards the car park. When Lilly reached the promenade, she was stunned. Trellis tables had been erected down the middle of the road, and a band was warming up outside the Blue Seagull pub.

Lilly felt an arm around her shoulders, guiding her towards the wake. 'Prue said you'd be here on your own and asked me to look out for you. I'm Martyn, proprietor of the Blue Seagull. We have spare rooms for tonight if you'd like to stay over.'

Martyn released Lilly, and she turned around to

face him. He'd been one of the pallbearers. Martyn had taken his jacket and black tie off, and he looked a lot younger. Lilly guessed he was mid-thirties as she surveyed his messy brown hair and sparkling green eyes. Lilly held out her hand. 'I'm Lilly. I'm pleased to meet you, Martyn. I'm not sure if I'm staying over. I don't know anyone. I must admit I feel a bit out of place.'

Martyn rubbed his chin. 'Well, we'll soon change that. Come with me, I'll introduce you to Ben and Bertie. They're two of Prue's "eligible bachelors". Ben's the local lawyer, his office is above Mrs Craddock's Tea Room, over there.' Lilly looked up at the *Ben Crenshaw – Lawyer* lettering on the windows above the tea room.

Ben emerged from the Blue Seagull, carrying two pints of beer, he handed one to Martyn. Lilly guessed he was late twenties. He was more polished than Martyn with short dark blonde hair and hazel eyes. Ben smiled at Lilly. 'You must be Lilly Lavender, your grandmother told me all about you.'

Another man bounded out of the pub carrying two glasses of champagne, he handed one to Lilly. 'Hi, my name's Bertie Chancery-Lorne, and I own the Estate Agents. I'm thirty-two, single, and on the lookout for a young lady with Prue's sense of humour.'

Lilly laughed. 'I think Granny Prue has set me up

here. Are you all single?'

Three smiling faces nodded at her.

The remaining pallbearer tapped Lilly's shoulder and she spun around, her long brown hair flying behind her. 'Hello, Lilly. My name's Miles. I'm pleased to meet you.'

Lilly's violet eyes looked up to the sky. 'Granny! This is so embarrassing; how could you do this to me?'

The lead singer of the band took to the microphone. 'Prue would like to thank you all for coming here today. She wants the best wake ever, and she would like her granddaughter, Lilly, to take to the floor for the first dance. It's one of Prue's favourites: *Wake Me Up Before You Go Go,* originally performed by the masters of Pop music *Wham.*'

Ben took the champagne flute from Lilly, and Miles stepped forward. 'May I have this dance?' He guided her onto the boarded floor outside the pub before whispering into her ear: 'I'm married. Your grandmother ran out of choice, so I had to fill in. They needed at least four men to carry her coffin. Prue was quite a woman. I'm sure she'll be loving all of this. Just try to look like you're enjoying it.'

Lilly began to relax. This was only a bit of fun, and it was what Granny Prue wanted. Who was she to spoil her grandmother's wake?

As soon as the song ended, Miles led Lilly to the table where the others were sitting. Lilly liked Miles; he made her feel at ease. It helped that he wasn't single like the others; that took the pressure off. She wasn't surprised Miles was married, with his light blonde hair and steel-blue eyes, he was the best looking of the bunch.

The girl sitting next to Martyn waved to Lilly. 'Come and sit over here, Lilly, I've saved you a seat. I'm Melissa and I work in the pub with my much older brother for my sins.'

Martyn nudged Melissa. 'There are only seven years between us, you make me sound ancient!'

Lilly laughed, she warmed to Melissa straight away. 'Martyn mentioned there are rooms available above the Blue Seagull tonight. Would it be OK if I book one?'

'Of course. Just let me know when you want to unpack, and I'll pop inside to get you a key.'

By eight o'clock, the sea breeze was picking up, and the wake was drawing to a close. Lilly was pleased that the weather for April had been warm enough to stay outside for so long. Martyn was now behind the bar in the pub, and Melissa had gone to get a room key for Lilly. Miles, as a doctor, had been called away earlier to deal with an emergency at the hospital. However,

Ben and Bertie were keen to keep Lilly company for the rest of the evening, and she was grateful for that. She said she'd meet them inside the pub once she'd collected her overnight bag from her car.

Lilly took time to reflect on the day as she strolled along the promenade on her way back to the Blue Seagull. What a whirlwind it had been. How did Granny Prue know so many people? What did Mrs Carmichael mean when she said that Prue was "crafty"? Why did Lilly's grandfather disappear? One thing was for sure, Lilly felt more in touch with her grandmother now than when she was alive. Lilly had a feeling that Granny Prue had more items left on her bucket list and that she, as her granddaughter, was the only person she trusted to cross them off.

3

WHERE THERE'S A WILL THERE'S A WAY

The following morning, Lilly sat in the restaurant area of the Blue Seagull eating her breakfast when she noticed Ben Crenshaw waving through the window. She stared at him as he mouthed the words 'May I join you?' Lilly nodded, and a smiling Ben breezed in to sit opposite her. Ben signalled to the waiter: 'My usual, please.'

Lilly poured another cup of tea from the pot and stared suspiciously at Ben, who couldn't contain his excitement any longer. 'I didn't feel it appropriate to discuss this yesterday, Lilly, but you can't go home until I've advised you of the contents of your grandmother's Last Will & Testament. I suggest that when you've finished your breakfast, we head over to my office so that we can speak in private.'

The waiter placed a coffee in front of Ben. 'I'll put it on your tab, Ben. Have a good day!'

Ben's hazel eyes had a mischievous look about them as he stared at Lilly over the rim of his coffee cup. Lilly focused on finishing her breakfast while trying to think of what could be in Granny Prue's Will. As far as she could remember, Granny only had a few ornaments in her cottage at Moonbeam Mews. Lilly presumed she'd taken them with her to the nursing home. Now, there was a thought. Who had picked up Granny's things from the nursing home? Lilly spread marmalade on the remaining piece of toast and made a mental note to ask Ben that question when they got to his office.

Breakfast finished; Lilly stood up. 'I'd best check-out of my room before we go to your office, please excuse me while I pop upstairs to get my bag.'

Melissa appeared on the scene. 'There's no need to check-out yet, Lilly. Your room isn't booked for tonight. Take as long as you need with Ben. You can catch up with me later.'

Ben stood up and opened the restaurant door. 'Let's go, Lilly. As soon as we get this done, you can get on with your life.'

*

'You are kidding me!' Lilly paced around Ben's office. 'Granny owned Pink Pomegranate Perfumery! They fired me two weeks ago.'

'That's correct.'

'Did Granny get me fired?'

Ben's eyes twinkled. 'That's open to interpretation. Your grandmother had plans for the business, but she ran out of time before she could bring them to fruition. She certainly didn't want you losing your job when the business moved to Starminster. So, I guess she gave you a little push ahead of time to see if you'd sink or swim.'

Lilly continued pacing. 'Oh, I sank, all right. I definitely sank. I'm young, free, and jobless. Great combination, don't you think?'

'That may not be for long.'

'What do you mean?'

'Your grandmother has left Pink Pomegranate Perfumery to you in her Will. However, there is a condition: You need to manage the transfer of the business from Tillingtree to Starminster. If you succeed with that, then the business will be yours. I have been chosen to monitor your progress and ensure the company remains profitable. I think your grandmother's words to me were "make sure there's no slacking". You will need to report to me weekly with progress and of course, as your lawyer, I am available at all times with any help and advice you may require.'

'Does that mean I will need to move down here?'

'I believe that is what your grandmother wished. She also hoped that you would move into Moonbeam Mews.'

'Moonbeam Mews! I've heard it's derelict.'

'Well, two of the cottages are in a state of neglect, but your grandmother's cottage has undergone a complete refurbishment in recent months. For some reason, Miss Lavender was completely attached to Moonbeam Mews. She fought a fierce battle to stop the cottages from being demolished. She bought the two that became vacant, and the profits from the perfumery went into the renovation fund. Unfortunately, she didn't live long enough to see the project through.'

Lilly sighed. 'Don't tell me. Granny wants me to manage the renovation of Moonbeam Mews too?'

Ben smiled. 'I know this will be a lot for you to take in, Lilly. But your grandmother was determined that her dreams would come true. If you are the channel via which she can achieve that, then maybe that's not a bad thing. I think both projects sound quite exciting. It won't be a straightforward renovation of the cottages; Miss Lavender has been granted planning permission to have the two remaining cottages converted into the new premises of the perfumery.'

Lilly slumped down in a chair. 'Miss Lavender. You keep calling her Miss Lavender. *I'm* Miss Lavender. I'm Miss Lilly Prudance Lavender. I can't get my head around Granny Prue being a "Miss". If I'm going to do this, you need to stop calling her by what I deem to be *my* name. You can call my Granny by the more acceptable name of "Prue".'

Ben held out his hand to shake Lilly's. 'If that's the only criteria that's stopping the deal, then I am more than happy to abide by it.'

Lilly narrowed her eyes before holding out her hand. 'You *will* help me, won't you, Ben Crenshaw? This is all quite scary.'

Ben held Lilly's hand in both of his. 'You've nothing to worry about, Lilly. Everyone's here to help. Just view it as the next chapter in your life. Prue has everything lined up for you to go on an amazing adventure.'

Lilly leant on Ben's desk. 'I don't know where to start. What do I do first?'

Ben handed Lilly a set of keys. 'Here are the keys to No. 1 Moonbeam Mews: your grandmother's cottage. Miles has advised me that he will meet you there at eleven o'clock this morning. He has Prue's remaining possessions; he picked them up from the nursing home.'

Lilly stood up and winked at Ben. 'I'd best get a move on then; I wouldn't want to be viewed as "slacking".'

4

A NEW LIFE

As Lilly approached Moonbeam Mews, she noticed Miles sitting on the wall outside, holding a box. He stood up as soon as he saw her. 'Lilly, I am here on your grandmother's instruction. She said I had to meet you at Moonbeam Mews with her possessions and she would be extremely cross if I didn't turn up. So here I am.'

Lilly managed a small laugh. 'What is there about Moonbeam Mews, that was so special to Granny? It should have been an unhappy place for her. My grandfather said he would meet her here, and he never turned up.'

Miles raised his eyebrows. 'Is that so? Prue always loved it here. She had big ideas for the place after she moved into the nursing home. There were some fierce battles with the Council about her plans for the renovation of the cottages which, of course, she won. Your grandmother was an amazing woman.'

Lilly nodded to the box. 'Are you holding Granny's possessions?'

'Yes. There aren't many. Prue gave her ornaments to her friends at the nursing home and arranged for her clothes to go to the charity shop. So, whatever's left in here, she especially wanted you to have.'

Apprehension washed over Lilly; she hadn't been in her grandmother's cottage for many years. She wondered if it would remind her of her childhood holidays; would the cottage still smell of Granny's gardenia soap? Lilly pushed the key into the lock. 'Will you come inside with me, Miles? This all seems surreal. Just two days ago I didn't even know that Granny had died, let alone left me her cottage and her perfumery.'

Miles followed Lilly inside, and she opened the shutters to reveal a modern fully furnished interior with a vase of lilies on the coffee table and a card which read:

To Lilly Lavender,

Welcome to Moonbeam Mews.
The fridge is stocked.

From your friends and neighbours
in Starminster x

Lilly looked at Miles, who placed the box on the floor next to the sofa and stood with hands on hips while he surveyed the pristine interior of the cottage. 'I heard they were doing this. Ben let Melissa in with the food and flowers. They're a friendly lot around here.'

Lilly wandered around the cottage in a daze. It was nothing like she remembered. The bedrooms upstairs were no longer dark and dreary; the walls were painted white, and the carpets were pale grey. Two of the bedrooms were empty, but the main bedroom had an exquisite silver bed and ash furniture. The curtains and bed linen were white with sprigs of lavender embroidered on them. The ancient bathroom was now light and airy with freestanding bath and walk-in shower cubicle. It was downstairs though that had taken on the main transformation. The former dark wood kitchen was now white and silver, with an island in the centre; and the lounge and dining room had been knocked through, making a large living area with views of both the promenade and the sea.

Miles smiled at Lilly. 'What do you think of your new home?'

Lilly looked out of the front window at the Blue Seagull pub over the road, and then walked across the room to look out of the side windows at the ocean. 'This is going to sound a horrible thing to say, but it doesn't feel like Granny Prue's house anymore. It feels like a whole new home; a home that's perfect for me.

This can't be happening – tell me it's not a dream.'

Miles picked up a packet of clotted cream biscuits from a food hamper on the kitchen work surface. 'It's definitely not a dream. These are my favourites; Prue always had a tin of biscuits to hand when I visited her at the nursing home. I'd say that she's ticked another item off her bucket list if she's turned her home into a modern version for you. I believe she was around your age when she first moved in here. Now two generations on she's allowing you to follow in her happiness.'

'Was she happy, Miles? Was Granny Prue happy?'

'Prue was always happy. Let me ask you the same question. Are you happy, Lilly?'

Lilly wrung her hands together as she looked to the floor. 'I don't think I've ever been truly happy. I've sort of lost my way.'

Miles looked around the kitchen. 'Mind if I put the kettle on? Prue always insisted I dipped her clotted cream biscuits into a mug of strong tea. You should try it; I certainly feel happy when I do it. If you choose to move to Starminster, I can guarantee that Prue's happiness will rub off on you. You'll discover lots about her that you never knew.'

Lilly felt a weight lifting from her shoulders and a feeling of excitement warming her heart. 'Go on then, you make the tea, and I'll find a plate for the biscuits.'

When the tea was poured from a silver teapot, Lilly reached for Granny Prue's box of possessions and placed it on the island in the middle of the kitchen. She sat down with Miles on the bar stools and before dunking a clotted cream biscuit, she lifted the lid of the box. It contained a large envelope with Granny Prue's writing on the front: MY ADVICE FOR LILLY.

Lilly laughed, and her violet eyes shone. 'Trust Granny to come up with a surprise.' She tore open the envelope and removed a selection of smaller ones.

'The envelope on top says "APRIL". The next one says "MAY". Maybe I'm supposed to open them in certain months. Shall I open the "APRIL" one now?'

Miles dunked his biscuit. 'I'm intrigued. Let's see what Prue's got to say.'

> *You will commence the first chapter of your happy ever after. There are opportunities before you. Embrace them. Don't shine in secret.*

Lilly reached for a biscuit. 'Well, it looks like Granny's determined for me to be happy. This may be just what I need to get focused and make something of my life.'

Miles dunked his fourth biscuit. 'What were you

saying earlier about a perfumery?'

'Oh, Granny owned a perfumery in Tillingtree, two hours from London. I worked there for six years, and I got the sack two weeks ago.'

'Well, I never. Prue never mentioned owning a perfumery, that will be a surprise to the locals. Did she sack her only grandchild?'

'No! Well, not directly. I didn't know she owned the perfumery until this morning. It's part of the deal with me moving into Moonbeam Mews that I manage the relocation of the business from Tillingtree to Starminster. Granny's already got planning permission for me to run the business from the two empty cottages next door. I've got to manage the redevelopment of them too.'

'It sounds like you're going to be busy! What's the name of the business?'

'Pink Pomegranate Perfumery.'

'Really!'

'Have you heard of it before?'

'My wife received a box of their products last week. It arrived out of the blue. She loves them. She'll be delighted you're going to run the business from here. That reminds me. Amanda has asked me to invite you to tea with her at three o'clock this afternoon. You'll easily find the cottage, it's next to St Mary's church on the hill, and it's called "Little-Bee-Lost", the name's on the gate.'

Miles grinned. 'Before you ask, it used to be my grandparents' home; I grew up there. I found a little bee that was drowning in a puddle one day when I was two. I rescued it, hence the cottage getting its name. I really must dash now. I'm due at the hospital in half an hour. Shall I let Amanda know you're available this afternoon?'

'Oh, please do, Miles. That's so kind of her. I know where your cottage is, we walked past it many times when I was younger. We came here every year for our holidays. I always loved the name.'

Lilly shut the door behind Miles and breathed in the scent of lilies. She closed her eyes and whispered, 'Thank you, Granny Prue. You've given me a new life. I promise I won't let you down.'

5

THE DOCTOR'S WIFE

Amanda Herriot could best be described as "magnificent". A former model, now self-styled fundraising legend, Amanda was the jewel in the crown of Starminster. Her irrepressible charm that extracted large donations from organisations all over the country, which she gave to good causes, granted her the persona of a modern-day Robin Hood.

The Herriot's lived in Little-Bee-Lost Cottage on the hill next to St Mary's Church. As far as cottages went, it was large, thatched and in four acres of land. At three o'clock precisely, Lilly rang the doorbell.

'Lilly Lavender! I'm so pleased to meet you. Do come in.'

Lilly shook hands with Amanda before manoeuvring her way around a set of designer luggage in the hallway.

Amanda noticed Lilly's curiosity. 'I travel a lot. I arrived back this morning, and I'm off again tomorrow. It was hardly worth dragging the whole lot upstairs in my condition.' Amanda patted her bulging stomach.

'You're pregnant! How lovely. When's the baby due?'

'September and it's twins. We've been trying for a few years and then two come along at once. Miles is ecstatic, bless him. I've already said we'll need a nanny or two when they arrive; my lifestyle doesn't allow for endless nappy changing and sleepless nights. Still, I'm doing my bit to provide heirs to the Herriot Heritage so to speak.'

Lilly followed Amanda into the kitchen. She was stunning. Her short pale blonde hair and baby blue eyes were striking enough, but the way she stood tall and walked as if on a catwalk, even with her bump, gave her an air of something akin to a goddess.

'Your husband mentioned you undertake charity work.'

Amanda gestured for Lilly to sit down at the kitchen table. 'Let's just say that my modelling career has given me an advantage of mingling with the rich. I do still model on occasions, but Miles isn't as supportive as he should be.'

Lilly huffed. 'Well, in my opinion, I think you should be allowed to do whatever you want. It's obvious you're suited to modelling. If I looked like you, I'd make the most of my assets. As Granny Prue would say: "Don't shine in secret". I bet you'd be even more in demand at the moment with your baby bump; you look terrific.'

Amanda pushed a plate of rice cakes in front of Lilly and sipped her mint tea. 'I like you, Lilly. I struggle to get girlfriends, particularly in a village like this. Women are jealous of me. Why aren't you jealous?'

Lilly reached for a rice cake. 'Well, I may have been jealous that you have such a good-looking husband, but now I know he's chauvinistic I'm amazed that you march to his tune. When I get married, I want to retain my identity. I want a man who will accept me for who I am.'

'And, who are you, Lilly?'

'I'm not sure yet. I've been lost for years. I'm hoping Granny Prue will sort me out.'

'But your grandmother is dead, Lilly.'

'Of course, I know that, but I have a feeling that Granny has my best interests at heart. I feel closer to her now than ever, and she's already changing my life for the better. I have a new home – her old one – and a business. That used to be hers too.'

'Doesn't it feel odd that you are following in some old woman's footsteps?'

'Not at all. It's as if Granny started something but didn't finish it, and I'm getting the opportunity to lead an even richer life than she did – which in itself will be quite an achievement.'

A sizeable watercolour painting on the kitchen wall caught Lilly's eye. 'Is that an original painting? It looks like it's signed.'

Amanda sighed. 'I can't stand that painting, but Miles won't let me throw it out. His grandfather was fascinated by pomegranates. Not only did he grow them in a greenhouse, but he also painted pictures of them. He was obsessed. I managed to remove most of them to the loft, but Miles insisted on keeping that one on the wall in memory of his grandfather.'

Lilly smiled. 'It's a small world. I have a connection with pomegranates too. Well, I used to work for Pink Pomegranate Perfumery in Tillingtree until two weeks ago.'

Amanda's baby blue eyes widened. 'Well, I never. I am awfully close to Mr Ling, the owner of the perfumery. He's an absolute delight. He's taken me to China Town on several occasions when I'm in London. It's such an eye-opener sharing authentic Chinese cuisine and entertainment with Mr Ling.'

A shudder encompassed Lilly. 'How did you meet Mr Ling?'

'Oh, he's a supporter of London Fashion Week. He came last year with a large supply of perfume and air fresheners for the girls and guys. He's so generous with freebies. He sent me a huge hamper of products just last week. He's definitely a fan of mine.'

Lilly felt sick. It wasn't the horrible, cardboard-textured, rice cake she'd just eaten – it was the thought of Mr Ling's double life. He wasn't the owner of the perfumery; Granny Prue was – or rather, Lilly was. Mr Ling worked in the storeroom and had obviously been syphoning off stock to give to Amanda and everyone at London Fashion Week! There was nothing else for it. Lilly needed to go to Tillingtree to sort things out. She hadn't been looking forward to seeing her old boss, Stefan, again. He'd fired her for no good reason. Still, she'd have to face the music sooner rather than later and have the courage to fire him when she announced the business was moving to Starminster. Lilly closed her eyes and wished: *Give me strength, Granny. Please give me strength. I don't know if I can do this.*

A chair screeched on the kitchen tiles as Amanda stood up to rinse her cup. 'Are you all right, Lilly? Have I bored you so much that you've fallen asleep?'

Lilly opened her eyes with renewed enthusiasm. 'I'm sorry, Amanda. I've just remembered there's something I need to do urgently. Please excuse me. It's been brilliant meeting you. Remember, be your own woman, don't let your light be snuffed out by a man. I must dash now. You've been very helpful, informative, err enlightening. Yes, that's it: Enlightening.'

Lilly waved as she strode towards the door. 'Don't worry; I'll let myself out. Just put your feet up and relax. Try a squirt of Pink Pomegranate's Vanilla Mist. That will calm you. See you soon!'

Amanda shook her head. Weird girl. Still, maybe she had a point; Miles shouldn't have stopped her glamour modelling when they first met. Amanda was now condemned to the occasional dull catwalk appearance. As Lilly's grandmother would say: "Don't shine in secret." Amanda reached for her little black book. The tabloids would be delighted she was back on the scene; a pregnancy shot of Amanda Herriot, doctor's wife, would be in high demand. Amanda could name her fee and Miles wouldn't mind when he saw the bank balance.

6

UNFINISHED BUSINESS

The following morning, Lilly stormed through the revolving doors of Pink Pomegranate Perfumery. Cara, the receptionist, looked up from her magazine. 'Lilly! What are you doing here?'

Lilly was in no mood for small talk. 'I've come to see Stefan.'

'He's in a meeting at the moment; you can't go in there.'

Lilly ignored Cara and burst into Stefan's office. Mr Ling's niece, Suki, was sitting on Stefan's lap. Lilly wasn't surprised. She'd worked as Stefan's Executive Assistant for six years and was accustomed to his womanising. Come to think of it; she'd been the one doing all the work and Stefan had just been fronting things up by taking customers out to dinner. He wasn't in control of what was going on in the business, or he would have discovered Mr Ling's misdemeanours. Lilly had flagged up to Stefan, on several occasions, that stock coming in from China wasn't tying up with the sales figures in the UK. With what she now knew, it tied in with Mr Ling and his niece joining the business last year.

Clarity flowed into Lilly's mind: Granny Prue knew about the collusion and corruption in her business. That's why she was moving it to Starminster and entrusting it with Lilly. A calmness encompassed her, and she sat down in a chair opposite Stefan and Suki.

'We can make this easy, or we can commence criminal proceedings. It's up to you. I am now the owner of this business, and I am closing it down with immediate effect. As far as I'm concerned, there are illegal goings-on from the top down. You are both fired. Collect your personal belongings and exit the premises immediately.'

Lilly stood up and turned around to see Mr Ling and an open-mouthed Cara in the reception area. 'I suppose you heard all of that. You're both fired too. I have evidence of Mr Ling syphoning off the company's products, and I have, for a long time, wondered why Cara is doing a boring job when she could do much better. Don't shine in secret, Cara. This is a deadpan company. It's not exactly thriving, is it?'

Suki and Mr Ling fled off to the storeroom to collect their possessions and Stefan sauntered out of the building with his wallet and phone. He didn't give Lilly a second glance.

Cara handed Lilly the keys to the building. 'This is just the push I needed, Lilly. I've been bored out of my mind for years.' Lilly noticed Cara walking away with a large carrier bag full of perfume. She turned a blind eye; the receptionist was as bad as the rest of them.

Lilly wandered around the empty building with a feeling of karma and excitement. There was so much she could do to improve the business when she'd relocated it to Starminster. Realisation then hit her that it wasn't just the business she was excited about; it was her new home, friends, and neighbours. For once in her life, she felt part of a community.

The thought of the six-hour drive two days in a row didn't bother her. Lilly just wanted to get "home" to Starminster. She'd go back to her apartment and pack as many clothes and possessions as she could into her car. That would be a start for now. Her new life was underway.

*

It was seven o'clock in the evening before Lilly arrived

back in Starminster. She parked outside Moonbeam Mews and unlocked the door of her cottage before going back to her car to offload her belongings.

Melissa watched Lilly from the window of the Blue Seagull pub. 'I'm just popping over the road, Martyn. Lilly's back, thank goodness.'

Lilly was struggling to carry armfuls of clothes on hangers into her lounge. Melissa reached onto the back seat of the car to help her. 'It's good to see you, Lilly. Where have you been? We've all been worried about you.'

Lilly frowned. She wasn't used to people asking where she was. 'Oh, I just popped up to Tillingtree to get some clothes and a few other bits.'

Melissa sighed. 'Well, you should have let us know where you were going. Ben and Miles have both been looking for you. You were last seen yesterday at about four o'clock leaving Little-Bee-Lost Cottage, and now you turn up again after having driven for what must be over twelve hours in just over a day. You will be shattered. Once we've emptied your car, you must pop over to the pub for dinner. No excuses, it's on the house. I'll let the boys know you're home.'

*

Martyn emerged from behind the bar carrying three bowls of pasta for Lilly, Miles, and Ben. Lilly sipped the cider that Melissa had poured for her, and she felt an overwhelming sense of happiness. She smiled with contentment. Ben couldn't help laughing. 'Look at you, what a transformation, you look like a cat that's got the cream.'

Lilly's twinkling violet eyes stunned Miles. 'You have a look of your grandmother. A hidden craftiness. What have you been up to?'

Lilly placed her fork on the table and leant back in her chair. 'I've closed Pink Pomegranate Perfumery in Tillingtree and sacked all the staff.' Lilly reached into her bag for the keys Cara gave her and waved them in the air. 'See! I saw them all off the premises and locked it up.'

Ben rubbed his chin. 'Things aren't that easy, Lilly. We need to take it slow and make sure we cover off any legal implications with the business relocating to Starminster. What if any of the staff are willing to move with the business?'

Lilly raised her shoulders. 'Well, I wouldn't want any of them. They're all corrupt, and I told them so. They accepted their fate without complaining. It was only a question of time before they got caught out. It was Amanda that drew my attention to fraud within my business yesterday.'

Miles's steel-blue eyes popped. '*My* Amanda?'

Lilly nodded as she savoured her dinner. She swallowed before she spoke. 'Yes. It was a good job your wife was at London Fashion Week last year, or I would never have known that the storeroom manager of my business was giving away our products, or that his niece was having an affair with the boss. My ex-boss to be precise. No wonder he let Granny fire me; I was just in the way. A goodie, goodie, when he was such a baddie. And then there was the receptionist – I'd known for years that she'd been waltzing off with air fresheners, candles and the like.'

As she came up for air, Lilly noticed the stunned faces opposite her. 'So, all in all, I've had a good day. Do you have a slot available in your diary tomorrow, Ben? We need to discuss the next steps of the business transfer. Also, Miles, I need to speak to you about pomegranates. I believe your grandfather used to grow them.'

7

THE ART OF POMEGRANATES

One week later, Miles climbed the ladder to his loft in Little-Bee-Lost Cottage and Amanda couldn't contain her delight.

'I like Lilly. She's got some "get up and go". Trust her to realise the potential in your grandfather's artwork. It's a brilliant idea they line the walls of her new shop. Maybe we could give her the painting in the kitchen too; then she'll have a full set.'

Miles peered down from the loft hatch and winked at Amanda. 'Nice try, but I'm keeping that one, it was my grandfather's favourite. I remember his passion for pomegranates from my childhood days. I like to keep a sense of who I am and where I've come from.'

Amanda sighed, 'If you must. What time are you going over to Lilly's? I've promised to meet Bertie for lunch at the Blue Seagull; he's sponsoring my latest charity project. It'll be a win-win for him, great publicity for the Estate Agents and the opportunity to spend a vast amount of time with me.'

Miles laughed; Amanda was as witty as she was beautiful. 'I need to be at Lilly's by eleven, Ben's joining us. Those two have been locked away all week working on the transfer of the perfumery. Ben sounded quite excited about it when I spoke to him. Lilly's surpassing herself with ideas. Prue would be delighted.'

'Ah, that's such great news. Make sure you join in and help them out. As you've always said to me: "It's good to play a part in the community". And, before you say it, I know you're a busy doctor, but you need to be doing something worthwhile in your spare time. Spend as much time as you need with Lilly. I'm hoping that once her business is up and running in Starminster, she'll be as benevolent as Mr Ling with donating her products to my good causes.'

*

Miles struggled to park near Moonbeam Mews; there were vans outside, and a skip had just been delivered. Miles popped his head around Lilly's open front door. Her brown hair was piled high on her head, and she was wearing white dungarees. She did a twirl. 'Do you like them? Granny sent them to me last Christmas. I never thought I'd wear them, but they will be great for painting in – not that there will be much painting to do for another two months. The builders have promised to pull out all the stops though to complete their work by July, so I'm planning a 1st of August opening.'

Miles smiled. 'Wow! That's a pretty impressive timescale. You've had a very productive week with Ben.'

Ben called out from the kitchen. 'Come on in, Miles. I've just made a pot of tea and, as luck would have it, I've got to dash off to deal with an urgent matter for a client who I've managed to avoid all week.'

Miles's heart sank; he didn't know why. Ben appeared to have made himself at home in Moonbeam Mews. He also squeezed Lilly's shoulders on the way out. Why should Miles feel annoyed about that?

Lilly pulled her arm from behind her back and presented Miles with a packet of clotted cream biscuits. 'Go on. Eat as many as you like. I won't tell Amanda.'

Miles took the biscuits but couldn't shake off a feeling of irritation. Lilly sensed his distant mood, so she tried to lift his spirits. 'Anyway, I'm glad Ben had to dash off because we're into May now and I have another envelope from Granny to open. As she gave you her box of messages to give to me, I feel it only appropriate that I open all of them with you – on the designated months, of course.'

Miles warmed to Lilly's exuberance and dunked a biscuit. The twinkle in his eyes alerted Lilly she had won him over. 'But before we do that, we need to finish our tea and then put our hard hats on. We can take a peek into next door to see how the building work is coming along and then we should collect your grandfather's paintings from your car.'

The inside of Numbers 2 and 3, Moonbeam Mews resembled a scene of mass destruction. Lilly winced. 'I must catch up with Mrs Carmichael about the work being done on her old property. I hope she doesn't mind. I'll make sure I take her a hamper of products once we're up and running.'

Miles glanced sideways at Lilly. 'I think Amanda will be leaning on your generosity for her charities.'

Lilly turned around, her eyes blazing in defiance. 'Oh, no, no, no. Mr Ling provided Amanda with enough free products to sink a ship. I have a business to start up and run. The projections show that I won't be in profit for ages. It's going to cost loads to get Pink Pomegranate Perfumery up and running again, and I need to be careful with the finances.'

'It sounds like you're really getting into this.'

'Oh, I am. Ben has been brilliant, and Bertie popped over the other night with a bottle of wine to give me advice on promotional materials. I'm getting lots of help.'

This was all becoming tiring for Miles. Lilly was a young woman with men falling at her feet. He shouldn't be bothered about that. But he was. 'I suppose Martyn will be inviting you out to dinner to discuss using your products in the guest rooms at the pub.'

Lilly blushed. 'Well, not dinner, but he's suggested I go over to the pub tonight to have a chat while he's working behind the bar. I'm presuming it's work-related, but you never know!'

There it was again, another pang of jealousy. Miles tried to analyse why, and he could only put it down to being young, free, and single. He'd been there, done that, and it wasn't as much fun as it was supposed to be. He was now married to a beautiful woman who was expecting his twins in four months. What more could he want? Miles had everything.

'Well, that's as much as we can see for now. It will be a different picture next month. It's going to be so exciting seeing it all being built from scratch. Let's go and get the paintings. I'll keep them safe in one of my bedrooms until the shop's ready, then they will take pride of place on the walls. It's so good of you to loan them to me. Would you mind if I get them re-framed, to go with my colour scheme?'

This previously sad, lost, young girl had turned into an entrepreneur in a matter of weeks. Miles felt genuine happiness for her. 'Go ahead. My grandfather would be delighted his work is displayed in Starminster for all to see. His passion for pomegranates lives on!'

After carrying the paintings upstairs and storing them in a spare bedroom, it was time to open Granny Prue's envelope for "MAY". Miles sat next to Lilly on the sofa in her lounge. 'Well, go on, open it then. I can't contain my suspense any longer.'

> *You will soon discover the secret of pomegranates. May my biggest regret become your greatest success.*

Lilly's eyes widened. 'Granny regretted buying the perfumery. I'm not surprised with the way it was being managed up in Tillingtree. Well, Granny needn't regret it anymore. I'll turn it into the success she always wanted. I'll do that for Granny Prue.'

Miles shuddered. He viewed Prue's words in a much different light. He needed to get back to Little-Bee-Lost Cottage to check something out. 'Well, your grandmother is certainly divulging some interesting information. I can't wait to hear what she has written for June. I must get off now, enjoy your date tonight with Martyn.'

Lilly laughed as she waved to Miles from her front door. 'Don't you go spreading rumours. It's not a date; it's just a drink and a chat.'

8

AN EVENING AT THE BLUE SEAGULL

Sitting on a barstool sipping a bespoke "Lilly Lavender" cocktail, Lilly couldn't help but compare Martyn's green eyes to a tropical paradise. They reminded her of numerous documentaries where the clearest of seas met with golden sand. Yes, Martyn's eyes could best be described as that; they were deep, clear, and stunning in colour. His messy brown hair suited him, and his figure-hugging white T-shirt left little to the imagination. Lilly was seeing Martyn in a new light.

Lilly leant on the bar. 'Do you try to impress all the girls by making them their own signature cocktails?'

Martyn blushed. 'No! I wasn't trying to impress, Lilly. I was just trying to be neighbourly, with you living over the road and all that.'

'Well, you've impressed me without even trying.'

The pub was filling up and a couple making their way into the restaurant caught Lilly's attention. 'Don't look now, but Alfie from the pasty shop has just walked in with Flora from the fish and chip shop. I bet you see lots of things going on from behind the bar.'

Martyn raised an eyebrow. 'Really? Thanks for letting me know. I missed that. You're right, I see all sorts of things from here.'

Lilly reached for her purse. 'I'll have another one of those delicious cocktails please and pour a drink for yourself. I'm paying.'

Melissa breezed through the bar leaving a trail of Chanel perfume. 'Hi, Lilly! Must dash, Ben's taking me to the Bistro in town tonight. Make sure that brother of mine keeps you entertained with his sparkling personality. If that fails, then try to drag out all the village gossip from him. He's a mine of information.' Melissa tapped a finger to her nose and waved before holding the door open for Bertie Chancery-Lorne to enter.

Bertie headed straight to the bar and sat down on a stool next to Lilly. 'I see Ben's still trying to win the affection of the magnificent Melissa.'

Lilly frowned. 'My lawyer's going out with Melissa?'

Bertie winked. 'Well, let's just say that there's a

shortage of eligible females in Starminster. Since you've turned up, the odds have gone up by fifty per cent. The lovely Amanda tries her best to help out, though – doesn't she Martyn?'

Martyn lowered his eyes. 'Don't listen to him, Lilly. He's still under the influence of too many whiskies from lunchtime.'

Lilly's head was spinning, and she stared at Bertie. 'Miles mentioned Amanda was having lunch with you today. I have to say that I'm not impressed with the way you're speaking about Melissa or Amanda and I suggest you go home now to sober up.'

Martyn's senses were on red alert, and he watched as Bertie leant towards Lilly. 'If I wanted to spend the evening sitting next to a wet lettuce, I could do that with one that doesn't have a potty mouth. I have a chilled bottle of chardonnay calling. Enjoy your evening, Miss Prim and Proper.'

As Bertie staggered out of the pub, Martyn glanced at Lilly. She didn't look hurt or embarrassed; she looked like she hadn't a care in the world. Lilly indeed held no blows. She'd managed to fire all the staff at the perfumery, and now she'd well and truly "sent off" Bertie. Martyn couldn't help but be impressed with Lilly's spirit.

Cheers and clapping emanated from the restaurant, and Lilly turned around to see Alfie kissing Flora. Her wide eyes met with Martyn's twinkling ones. 'It's their tenth Wedding Anniversary. Their friends and family booked a surprise party. Nice idea, don't you think?'

Lilly couldn't contain her laughter. 'I suggest you fill me in on as much gossip as you can. I need to know everything about this village before I put my foot in it.'

*

Back at Little-Bee-Lost Cottage, Miles stood in front of the pomegranate painting in the kitchen. He bent down and scrutinised the faintly scrawled message below his grandfather's signature. It was a message he'd first noticed after his grandmother had died when he was ten; he was certain it hadn't been there before. It didn't make sense at the time, and he'd thought no further of it, until now. The message read:

My one true love. I couldn't meet her at Moonbeam Mews. I had to do the right thing.

Clarity hit Miles like a ton of bricks . . . Miles's grandfather was Prue's lover. He didn't meet her at Moonbeam Mews because he was married. He'd planned to but had second thoughts. Prue's baby – Lilly's father – was Miles's uncle. No wonder there was a strong connection between Lilly and Miles. That was what Prue meant when she said that Lilly would "soon discover the secret of pomegranates". Miles slumped into a chair; no wonder he was so protective of Lilly –

she was his cousin.

*

Martyn was the perfect gentleman – not a word of gossip passed his lips. Instead, he turned the questioning around and asked about Lilly, whose life until now had been decidedly dull. With conversation lacking and Martyn serving customers, Lilly sent a text to Miles:

> *I'm dying of boredom in the pub. Did Amanda get back OK from her lunch with Bertie? He popped in here earlier, and he's as drunk as a skunk. I'd appreciate your help with choosing new frames for the paintings. Let me know when you can take a trip into town. Speak soon. Lilly*

Miles's heart sank. Amanda had called earlier to say that her lunch meeting with Bertie had carried over into dinner and she wouldn't be home until ten o'clock. It was eight forty-five now. It also wasn't the first time that Amanda was late home. Miles was tired of questioning her; she always had a well-prepared excuse. Was it so tedious being a doctor's wife that spending time at home was to be avoided at all costs?

Still, the babies were due in four months, Amanda must start slowing down soon, and once they were born, she'd be the perfect mother. Miles just needed to be patient, and everything would fall into place. He sent a text to Lilly:

> *My shifts for the next month are atrocious. Amanda wants me to decorate the nursery too. If you need the frames beforehand, then I trust your judgement. Martyn loosens up after a pint of Starminster Ale. Miles*

Lilly smiled, trust Miles to know how to break down Martyn's stiff exterior. She waved to him from the end of the bar. 'Two pints of Starminster Ale please.'

Martyn poured a pint and handed it to Lilly. 'One pint at a time. I bet you don't finish this one without having to be carried home.'

Lilly laughed. 'The other pint's for you, silly. I won't feel like a fully-fledged member of the community if the landlord of the Blue Seagull public house doesn't join me for my first pint of local beer. It will be quite an experience. I've never drunk beer before.'

Martyn pulled another pint with his green eyes set on Lilly. 'If you insist.'

Half a pint later, Lilly was struggling to concentrate on what a chatty Martyn was saying. 'Did you just say, "Amanda's a dark horse"? You'll need to back that up with factual evidence.'

Martyn took the glass away from Lilly. 'I said

nothing of the sort. Starminster Ale doesn't agree with you. I've won the bet; you couldn't even manage half a pint. I'll see you home safely; then I suggest you get an early night. You've had too much of my engaging company for one evening.'

9

SECRETS

The next four weeks passed in a whirlwind for Lilly. She'd been back to Tillingtree several times to clear out her apartment and arrange for the stock of Pink Pomegranate Perfumery to be transported to Starminster. Bertie Chancery-Lorne was most apologetic after his drunken rant in the pub, and he had suggested Lilly use the empty barn in the grounds of his property as a storeroom while the renovation work was being undertaken at Moonbeam Mews.

It had taken a while, but Lilly was warming to Bertie. With his black curly hair, blue eyes, and ruddy complexion, he personified a typical country gent. His yellow Ferrari parked in the grounds of Lorne House gave away the playboy side of his nature. He didn't care in the slightest that Martyn regularly mocked the colour by quipping that, "Ferraris should be red, and Porsches should be black". That might be Martyn's view, but Bertie wasn't perturbed by it in the least. A Ferrari was a Ferrari, no matter what colour it was. Martyn was just jealous.

After offloading the stock that had arrived from Tillingtree into Bertie's barn, Ben, Martyn, and Miles stood waiting for further instruction from Lilly.

'I can't thank you enough for helping me with all that lifting. Bertie's been a godsend with lending me his barn. If you're all available tonight, I'll buy you dinner in the Blue Seagull.'

Bertie and Ben jumped at the chance. Martyn confirmed that Melissa would cover for him for an hour and Miles said he'd need to check with Amanda. Lilly was happy with that. She said there was nothing further that needed doing that hot June afternoon except for Miles to take her into town to choose new frames for his grandfather's paintings. Bertie offered cold beers to Ben and Martyn, and they followed him into the back garden of the house.

Miles opened his car door for Lilly. 'I'm sorry you've had to wait for me to have some spare time to do this. I really wouldn't have minded if you'd chosen the frames on your own.'

Lilly fastened her seatbelt. 'That was never going

to happen. The paintings are only on loan to me, and I need your approval that I'm showing them off at their best. It doesn't end with choosing the frames – I'll need you to help me display them on the walls of the shop. How lucky is it that your grandfather had a passion for pomegranates, and my grandmother named her perfumery after them? It's such an amazing coincidence.'

Miles turned the key in his ignition and manoeuvred his car down the winding drive of Lorne House. He took a sideways glance at Lilly and chose his words carefully: 'It's not a coincidence, Lilly. My grandfather had a passion for your grandmother. So much so that he's your grandfather too. He's Prue's one true love that didn't turn up to meet her at Moonbeam Mews.'

Lilly sank back into her seat and twisted the frayed edges of her denim shorts. If Miles's grandfather had an affair with Granny Prue that produced Lilly's father, that meant she was related to Miles, who had just reached over to take her hand to stop her fiddling with her shorts.

'We're cousins, Lilly. I knew there was a strong connection between us, but I couldn't work out why.'

'How *did* you work it out?'

'The pomegranate painting in the kitchen. After

my grandmother died, my grandfather faintly scrawled a message under his signature. I don't think anyone has ever noticed. It caught my attention though, as it was at eye level for a ten-year-old. It didn't make sense to me at the time, in fact, I'd forgotten about it. That was until we read Prue's note last month.'

'What does the message say?'

'My one true love. I couldn't meet her at Moonbeam Mews. I had to do the right thing.'

Lilly sighed. 'Poor Granny, she was in love with a married man.'

Miles drove the car to a halt in the town car park. 'My grandfather should have known better, but I don't feel anger towards him. My grandparents were never suited to one another. I guess he did what he thought was the most decent thing at the time and that was to remain in a loveless marriage. Someone had to lose out, and that was Prue.'

Lilly undid her seatbelt and sobbed. Miles put his arm around her. 'We owe it to Prue to carry out her wishes now. She's obviously got some unfinished business. Come along, cousin, let's choose some frames then I'll drive you back to Moonbeam Mews. We need to get back to read your grandmother's words of wisdom for June.'

*

Lilly's vision for the shop was of the palest pink walls and white sparkle quartz floor tiles. Miles thought narrow silver picture frames would bring out the sparkle in the floor and gently enhance his grandfather's watercolours. Lilly couldn't agree more. The couple carried the frames upstairs and stored them in the bedroom with the paintings. Once back in the lounge, Lilly reached for Granny Prue's box of envelopes. She couldn't help but feel sad for her grandmother. It was fantastic news that she had a cousin in Starminster, she knew Miles would always look out for her, and that was a comforting feeling – but poor Granny Prue.

'OK, let's see what Granny has in store for us this month.' Lilly opened the envelope marked "JUNE".

> *Don't take the easy path. Take the right one. Never settle for second best. Keep secrets safe until they can be told.*

Miles looked at Lilly. 'That's obscure. Do you have any secrets?'

Lilly shook her head. 'You must know by now that I'm an open book. If I had a secret, it would be right out there. Have you got secrets?'

'Of course. Boy's code and all that. Also, in my line of work, I have to keep everything secret for patient confidentiality.'

Lilly laughed. 'Boy's code! I can't imagine you being one of the boys. You're always so right and proper when we're out in a group with the others.'

'Really? Is that how you see me? I'm just a boring, stuffy old doctor?'

Lilly punched Miles on his shoulder. 'A bit. How about I see a different side to you tonight, cousin?'

Miles looked at his watch. He needed to check with Amanda if it was OK for him to go out for dinner. He sensed Lilly was reading his thoughts.

'Well, it's five o'clock now. Why don't we get our appetite up by going for a stroll down the beach? I can leave my car here until the morning. A walk home up the hill after a few pints of Starminster will be just what I need later. Are you up for that, cousin?'

Lilly jumped up in delight. 'Definitely, cousin. On one condition.'

'What's that?'

'We need to stop calling each other "cousin". That's a secret we should keep between us for the sake of our grandparents.'

Miles held out his hand to shake Lilly's. 'It's a deal, Miss Lavender.'

10

'THANK YOU' MEAL

Having a secret cousin was the best thing that had ever happened to Lilly. Their connection was real and exciting. Miles could even read her thoughts. On their walk down the beach, he suggested they popped into Flora's shop to buy a small bag of chips to share before dinner. He poured salt and vinegar on them without even asking if Lilly liked salt and vinegar – she did.

Half-way down the beach Miles pointed to a block of apartments. 'That's where Mrs Carmichael lives. You wanted to let her know that you are demolishing her old home.'

Lilly stared at Miles whose usual combed to perfection light blonde hair was blown out of shape.

'How did you remember that? Do you know which apartment is hers?'

'Well, I'm not allowed to say due to doctor/patient confidentiality, but even you must recognise her sitting on that ground floor terrace.'

'Oh, how lovely! She's got lots of plant pots and a sea view. Let's go over and see her now.'

Mrs Carmichael was delighted to have visitors, if only for ten minutes. 'It is so kind of you, Lilly, to let me know what's going on at Moonbeam Mews. I find it all rather exciting! Thank you for inviting me to the party when the shop opens. I'll see you both soon.'

It was eight-fifteen before a windswept and giggling Lilly and Miles strolled into the Blue Seagull. Ben and Bertie were sitting up at the bar with Martyn behind it. Ben waved to attract their attention. 'You didn't mention a time, Lilly. So, we got here for eight.'

Lilly hugged Ben and Bertie and high-fived Martyn. 'We've had such a good afternoon. We got the frames for the paintings, and we've been to see Mrs Carmichael. It was bothering me that she didn't know what was going on with her old home. She's as excited about it as all of us now, and I need to arrange a party for the opening day as I've invited her to one!'

Miles chuckled and nodded to Martyn. 'A sauvignon blanc for Lilly, a pint of Starminster for me, and whatever you three are having. I just need to make a call.'

Martyn looked at Ben, who looked at Bertie, who looked at Lilly before asking the question: 'What have you done to Miles? We've not seen him like that for years.'

Lilly shrugged her shoulders. A sauvignon blanc? She knew it was a white wine, but she usually just asked for the "house" variety. Lilly was no connoisseur of wine. Still, Miles knew she wanted a bag of chips before dinner earlier, so maybe he knew something else about her that she hadn't yet discovered herself.

Miles checked his phone. There were no messages from Amanda. He had said he would be home mid-afternoon – she hadn't noticed he was late. Very late. Miles could only guess that she wasn't home either. After a pang of loneliness, he decided not to call her or to leave a message. Amanda wasn't bothered about him. If he thought about it seriously, he knew that. The twins were on their way, and Miles owed it to them to keep his marriage together. However, tonight was another matter – Miles was going to enjoy himself for the first time in a long time.

Lilly raised her glass in the air. 'I'd like to say thank you so much to all of you for your help this morning. I have now officially moved from Tillingtree to Starminster.'

Claps and cheers preceded an announcement from Ben: 'I must admit I am taken aback by how wholeheartedly you've thrown yourself into such a big lifestyle change. Prue would be delighted if she saw you now. Let's raise our glasses to Lilly!'

Lilly smiled. 'Oh, Granny Prue's still keeping an eye on me, I'm sure of that. I'm being driven on by her wise words.'

Bertie stared at Miles. 'Well, well, well, doctor. I haven't seen your blonde locks in such a state since we played rugby. We managed a fair few pints of Starminster in those days, didn't we?'

Miles closed his eyes as he savoured his pint and Martyn answered for him. 'Don't forget the cricket; even Ben played cricket. We should all take it up again. Why did we give it up in the first place?'

Ben laughed. 'Well, you got stuck behind the bar of this pub, Bertie became unfit, and Miles got married. It wasn't much fun for me playing with a load of youngsters, so I backed out gracefully. I must admit, I wouldn't mind playing again.'

Lilly clapped her hands in delight. 'I've just had the most brilliant idea! Amanda could organise a charity cricket match. A charity game wouldn't be too taxing for any of you; even Bertie should be able to manage that.' Lilly winked at Bertie.

Melissa sniggered from behind the bar. It was good to see her brother letting his hair down. Martyn worked far too hard. She didn't mind covering for him for the whole of the evening, and she poured another round of drinks to take over to the lively group.

After dinner, the friends moved to the bar area, and Miles challenged Lilly to a game of pool, which she won. Lilly nudged Miles before whispering, 'You let me win, didn't you? I've never won a game of pool in my life.'

Miles nudged her back. 'Well, you have now. You can cross that one off your bucket list.'

Lilly laughed. 'I don't have a bucket list, do you?'

Miles checked his watch; it was nearly eleven o'clock. 'No, I don't have a bucket list. Maybe we should start our bucket lists soon so that we don't run out of time like Prue. It's almost closing time, let me walk you home, then I'll head off up the hill. It's OK to leave my car at yours overnight, isn't it?'

Lilly and Miles said their goodbyes to everyone in the pub and headed over the road to Moonbeam Mews. Lilly opened her front door. 'What would you have on your bucket list if you had one?'

Miles rubbed his chin. 'Now let me think – to eat clotted cream biscuits every day for the rest of my life; to thrash Bertie at cricket; to remain more alert than

Martyn after four pints of Starminster – come to think of it I achieved that last one tonight. Have you any ideas for your bucket list?'

Lilly stepped inside her cottage and peered around the door to protect her embarrassment. 'I'd like to walk down the aisle to the Wedding March at St Mary's Church on the hill. I'd like to do that for Granny Prue. Now, off with you! Don't be noisy when you get home. Amanda needs her beauty sleep. Thank you for a lovely day.'

11

SCANDAL

Mrs Craddock's Tea Room was a hive of activity. The July edition of the Starminster Oracle had been delivered in bulk ready for distribution around the village by a regular group of volunteers. The only trouble was the opinion of the volunteers – on this occasion – was split.

Mrs Craddock poured tea by the cupful and mopped her brow with her apron. She carried platefuls of scones and cupcakes over to the regular customers and tourists who sat listening to the quarrelling going on in the back corner of the room: 'They should be burned if you ask me … I think they're rather tasteful … What on earth made her do it? … Well, I won't be the one posting this edition through the letterbox of Little-Bee-Lost Cottage.'

Melissa stood at the counter, waiting to be served.

'A fresh cream doughnut for me to take away please, Mrs Craddock. I need a sugar fix today.'

Mrs Craddock raised her eyes and nodded towards the bickering group. 'You'll never guess what Amanda's done now. She's gone and got herself a centre-page spread in the Oracle. There's not much left to the imagination. Can you believe it? What's Miles going to say? I'm pretty certain he won't know what she's been up to. It's not tasteful at any time, let alone in her condition. Everyone thought she'd turned a new leaf since getting married.'

Melissa paid for her doughnut and took a copy of the Oracle off the warring table. 'I've taken one of the pub's copies. I need to find a plumber in the small ads. Thanks, ladies and gents.'

Back at the Blue Seagull, Melissa felt sick. How could Amanda do this to Miles? Martyn grimaced. 'I'll speak to Ben; we need to stop them from distributing this straight away. The Oracle shouldn't be printing things like this.'

Ben couldn't find a legal issue with the photograph. It was tasteful to a degree – the worst thing was that it was a risqué portrayal of their close friend's pregnant wife.

Melissa called in to see Lilly. 'Lilly, the most dreadful thing has happened. Amanda has posed for the centrefold of July's Starminster Oracle and, trust me, she's not left much to the imagination. Miles is going to have a hissy fit; she promised him she'd given up glamour modelling.'

Lilly slapped a hand to her mouth. 'Glamour modelling? I thought she was a catwalk model.'

Melissa shook her head. 'What are we going to do, Lilly? Miles should never have married her; it was obvious she wouldn't change her ways. He's stuck with her now with the twins coming along. She's well and truly done it this time. We all kept quiet about her indiscretion over Christmas, poor Martyn's petrified the babies are going to have green eyes.'

It was now Melissa's turn to slap her hand to her mouth. 'Forget I said that, Lilly.'

Lilly felt enraged. 'How could Martyn do that to Miles?'

Melissa sighed. 'It wasn't totally his fault. Amanda spiked his drink.'

Lilly fell back onto her sofa and Melissa joined her. 'Who else knows about Martyn and Amanda?'

'Only Bertie, Ben, me, and now you.'

Lilly pulled at her hair. What a mess. She closed her eyes and tried to think of a solution, but she quickly concluded there wasn't one. How could she keep such a big secret from her cousin? Granny Prue's words were stamped on her mind as if they'd been written there in permanent ink: *Keep secrets safe until they can be told.*

Those words gave Lilly some comfort. Granny was right; it would be childish to go blabbing to Miles at the earliest opportunity. If the babies had blue eyes and Miles and Amanda worked through their differences about the centrefold blip, things could carry on as usual. Lilly rubbed her forehead as more of her Granny's words re-surfaced: *Don't shine in secret.* Lilly sat forward, head in hands, had Granny Prue wanted to get Amanda into trouble with Miles? Lilly removed that ridiculous thought from her mind. It was Lilly who had got Amanda into trouble, and now she needed to get her out of it.

Melissa jumped up. 'Come on, Lilly? What are we going to do? The volunteers are in Mrs Craddock's Tea Room now sorting out the Oracle for distribution to the whole of the village.'

Lilly headed for the door. 'We need to get over there, I'll think on the way.'

Lilly breezed into the tea room and walked straight over to the table heaving with copies of the offending magazine. 'Hello everyone, I'm Lilly Lavender, and I need your help.'

The volunteers stopped arguing and stared at Lilly, who smiled and continued with her plea. 'My new business, the Pink Pomegranate Perfumery, is due to open next month in Moonbeam Mews and I would be so grateful if I could insert an advertisement into the Starminster Oracle so that the whole village will know about it.'

One of the volunteers smirked. 'Well, you're too late, lovey. It's gone to print. Here it is, and we'll be distributing it tomorrow.'

Lilly continued to smile. 'Oh, I can see that. I was just thinking about producing a flyer to insert inside each magazine. I can't miss an opportunity like this.'

Another volunteer stared at Lilly through narrowed eyes. 'So, you're saying you want to advertise for free. You've got a damn cheek, young lady.'

Melissa hung her head, and Lilly blushed. 'Oh, I know it sounds awfully rude, but it really isn't. I'll clear things with the editor and give a donation.'

The first volunteer folded her arms. 'Well, I hope you're not going to ask us to insert your flyers, or even lug them around with the magazines. We're volunteers, you know. All that extra weight for us to drag around the village in our trolleys just isn't on.'

Lilly noticed the empty teacups and plates on the table. 'Let me buy you some more drinks and a selection of Mrs Craddock's lovely cakes. We can have a little chat to see if we can agree a deal.'

*

Two hours later Melissa and Lilly strode into the Blue Seagull, followed by a bemused Bertie. Ben had been summoned to the pub by Lilly twenty minutes earlier and Martyn emerged from behind the bar to join everyone at a table in the corner of the room.

Melissa glanced over her shoulder then spoke in a low voice. 'Lilly has managed to bribe the volunteers with hampers of Pink Pomegranate products; they won't be mentioning Amanda's fall from grace any time soon. She's also offered to distribute this month's Oracle herself. Bertie has been a brilliant help. He brought the hampers from his barn to the tea room and has now taken all the magazines to Lilly's cottage. So, we're amazingly in complete control of what goes out in the Oracle this month.'

Martyn and Ben let out sighs of relief and Lilly took over from Melissa. 'This is where I need your help. I have to produce some flyers to advertise my business, and I would appreciate it if Ben could print them off for me this afternoon. We should then meet at mine at six o'clock so that we can rip the centrefolds out of the Oracles and enclose my flyers. I then need your help with distributing the magazines to all households in the village tomorrow.'

Ben had a question. 'Does anyone know what shifts Miles is working this week? It will raise suspicion if he sees us all distributing Oracles around the village.'

It was now Lilly's turn to look over her shoulder. 'We've got that covered. Miles is working an early shift tomorrow, and Amanda is off on one of her charity missions. That means we need to finish the job by two o'clock.'

Martyn stared at Lilly, and she looked deep into his tropical green eyes, how could he do what he did to Miles? She cleared her thoughts. 'Do you have a question, Martyn?'

'Yes. What's Amanda going to say when she sees that she's missing from the Oracle?'

Lilly frowned. 'Leave that with me. I'll make her see reason. She'll thank me once she realises her mistake. I'll have to keep quiet about you all helping me, though. Once we've completed our mission, we can put it all behind us. Some secrets need keeping.'

12

MISSION NEARLY ACCOMPLISHED

By two-thirty the following afternoon, the group of friends were enjoying a late lunch in the garden of the pub. Ben slapped Martyn on the back. 'I can't believe we just did that! Miles certainly owes us all one.'

Lilly's mind was spinning. 'Is Mrs Craddock a gossiper? We've destroyed all the hard evidence and bribed the volunteers with freebies and a day off from work, but I forgot about Mrs Craddock.'

Melissa patted Lilly's arm. 'Don't worry, Mrs Craddock is very discreet. She hears so much about what's going on in the village in her tea room. People wouldn't go in there for a chat if they thought she couldn't be trusted. Besides, she's always had a soft spot for Miles; I'm sure we won't be the only ones protecting him from Amanda's latest escapade.'

An exhausted Lilly slumped back in her chair and closed her eyes, enjoying the sun's rays on her face. 'That's good then, well-done everyone, we did it!'

Bertie coughed, and silence preceded the sound of footsteps next to Lilly's chair. She opened her eyes to the sight of Miles. 'I don't know, I've just finished a strenuous early shift, and you're all lounging around in the pub garden. Is there any food for a very hungry doctor whose wife's away saving the world on one of her charity missions?'

Martyn and Melissa jumped up and cleared away the empty plates and glasses. Melissa pushed Miles into the chair next to Lilly. 'Sit down, doctor. That's our lunch break over. I'll get a menu for you.'

Melissa's conscience was pricking her. She hadn't wanted to worry Lilly, but Mrs Craddock and the regulars in the tea room loved a bit of gossip. She needed to divert attention away from Amanda onto something else.

The village postman handed the pub's mail across the bar to Martyn and peered into the garden. 'That's Prue's granddaughter out there, isn't it? We've had a large delivery for Prue today, and someone will need to drive round to collect it. There's a delivery from the

Oracle for Amanda Herriot too – looks like a large photo frame. I'll just pop out back and let them know.'

Ben and Bertie sat open-mouthed as Miles finished his lunch. 'What's up with you two? You look like you're fly catching. Either that or you wished you'd chosen that delicious steak pie I've just eaten for lunch.'

Miles chuckled, and Lilly sat in silence. All that hard work and now the Oracle had sent Amanda her very own blown-up photograph to display inside Little-Bee-Lost Cottage. Miles reached over and squeezed Lilly around her shoulders. 'Cheer up, Lilly. Your grandmother must have ordered something before she … before she left us. As I've got to pick up Amanda's delivery, I'll pick up Prue's too and drop it off at Moonbeam Mews.'

Bertie stood up. 'No! I mean there's no need. I'm on my way to the Post Office now, so I'll collect your deliveries and drop them off to you both.'

Lilly jumped up. 'I'll come with you; I can't wait to see what's arrived for Granny Prue.'

Miles ordered a coffee. 'Are you having one, Ben? I'm pleased that Lilly's slotted in so well in the community. It feels like she's been here forever.'

*

Bertie lugged four heavy boxes into Lilly's lounge, along with the large frame for Amanda. Lilly carried the package from the Oracle up to her spare bedroom and hid it behind the newly framed pomegranate paintings which were ready for the shop's opening next month.

Miles noticed the yellow Ferrari outside Moonbeam Mews and knocked on Lilly's door. Bertie opened it. 'I'm just on my way home up the hill. I can take the package for Amanda.'

Lilly stood at the top of the stairs as a red-faced Bertie pointed to the four large boxes in the middle of the lounge floor. 'There was a mistake – nothing for Amanda. Goodness knows what's in these boxes that Prue ordered. Nearly did my back in carrying them all. Must dash now. Need to get back to work.'

Bertie flew out of the door, and Lilly ran down the stairs. 'Oh, I'm so pleased to see you, Miles. You can help me unpack whatever's in these boxes.'

Miles watched as Lilly rushed around, plumping up the cushions on her sofa and straightening her tied-back curtains before rushing into her kitchen. His heart went out to her. She was being so brave about her grandmother's delivery. Miles hoped the boxes didn't contain anything that would upset Lilly.

Scissors in hand, Lilly cut through the parcel tape

on a box. Miles held his breath as Lilly pulled back the cardboard to reveal . . . books! Lilly knelt on the floor, and Miles joined her. The books were entitled: *STARMINSTER – Secrets Revealed, by Prudance Lavender.*

Miles punched the air and grinned from ear to ear. 'Prue did it! Your grandmother had so many stories to tell about her time in Starminster that I suggested she wrote a book about them. Prue promised me she'd do it. She even said she'd put it on her bucket list.'

Lilly was about to throw her arms around Miles when Melissa appeared in the open doorway. 'Hi, Lilly, did you get things sorted? Oh . . . hi, Miles.'

Lilly jumped up. 'All sorted, Melissa. Just look what Granny Prue's done. She's written a book about Starminster's secrets. I can't wait to read it, come in and have a look.'

Melissa picked up a copy and held it to her chest. 'Your grandmother was the most amazing woman I ever knew. What perfect timing! I'd like to buy ten of these books, Lilly. Can I take them now? I want to donate them to Mrs Craddock's tea room.' Melissa turned her back to Miles and winked at Lilly.

'What a great idea, Melissa. No need to pay for them. Take as many as you want to keep the regulars at the tea room occupied. Do you need a hand to carry them over? We can go now.'

'That's great, Lilly. Yesterday's news makes room for today's stories if you know what I mean. I can carry ten copies. I'll pop over there with them now. Thank you so much!'

Miles was reading the back cover. 'Would you mind if I buy a copy, Lilly?'

'Don't be silly, Miles. You can have one. You were Granny's inspiration. I'm just so pleased she managed to get published and that the books arrived today. How lucky was that?'

Miles raised an eyebrow and Lilly decided to stop chattering. She went into the kitchen to put the kettle on, and Miles followed her. 'You're doing really well, Lilly. It's difficult enough to lose someone you love without getting constant reminders of them. You need time to heal. I can't help but feel that Prue hasn't let go of this earth yet and is still living in some way through you.'

Lilly sighed. 'I know what you mean, Miles, but I feel that Granny is just holding my hand until I'm up and running on my own two feet. Grannies do that don't they? I find it rather comforting. I'll be at a loss once I've opened all her letters.'

'Well, we're in July now. Do you want to open her next letter today, or would you rather leave it a while?'

'July! Of course, it is. You make the tea, and I'll find

Granny's letter. There are some clotted cream biscuits in the top drawer on the right.'

Lilly opened the box Granny Prue had given to Miles in the nursing home. There were just two letters left: one each for July and August. Granny obviously thought Lilly would be well and truly up and running by then.

'Well, here it is. Let's see what wise words are in store for me this month.'

> *If it doesn't feel right, don't do it. Be aware of coming to the wrong conclusions. Honesty is the best policy.*

Lilly's cheeks burned, and Miles kept his gaze steadily on her. 'You've been acting strangely all afternoon. Is there something you want to tell me?'

Granny Prue's note burned Lilly's hand. She was sure it was conflicting advice compared to last month's message about keeping secrets until they could be told. It had felt the right thing to do to protect Miles's grandfather's infidelity with Granny Prue. Nothing could be done about that now. But, trying to protect Amanda was making Lilly feel extremely uncomfortable, particularly because all of this was her fault.

With Lilly choosing to remain silent, Miles helped her out. 'I saw Bertie carrying a large frame in here at the same time as the boxes. Amanda called me to say that he had signed for it at the Post Office. Are you going to tell me where it is?'

Lilly had nowhere to hide. She went upstairs to collect the frame. As she handed it to Miles, she said, 'I'm so sorry.'

Miles ripped at the brown paper wrapping. His eyes lit up when he saw the blown-up image, and he turned it around to show Lilly a scan picture of his twin babies. 'Amanda's friendly with the photographer at the Oracle and he arranged to have this done for us. It's brilliant, don't you think? Why were you hiding it?'

Lilly didn't know whether to laugh or cry. 'We thought it was meant as a surprise for you, Miles. I was going to give it to Amanda when she's back from her travels.'

Miles smiled. 'Well, there's no need now. I'll take it home with me, along with Prue's book. Thanks for the tea, Lilly, I'd best be on my way.'

13

MORE SCANDAL

Prue's book was proving to be a success in the tea room. With decades of secrets to read through, the regulars were enthralled: 'It's a good job old Jack's long since passed, along with his missus, that story's hilarious … My mother told me about New Year's Eve 1969 – she left that bit out though, scandalous! … Trust Prue to take up synchronised swimming in her fifties; I never knew that.'

Melissa and Lilly sat at a table sniggering as they flicked through the book. Lilly ate a forkful of lemon drizzle cake, and Melissa savoured her fresh cream doughnut before whispering. 'What a relief, Lilly. I can't believe we pulled it off. As far as Miles is concerned, Amanda's still as pure as the driven snow.'

Lilly felt the weight from her shoulders lifting. 'I didn't feel right about hiding Amanda's package from the Oracle. How lucky was it that Miles saw Bertie carrying it into Moonbeam Mews? Can you believe we all jumped to the wrong conclusion about it?'

The door to the tea room opened, and Amanda walked in, she saw Lilly and Melissa and headed straight for their table. 'May I join you?'

Lilly pulled out a chair. 'Of course. You look thoughtful, is anything the matter?'

Amanda stared at Lilly, then glanced at Melissa, who finished her doughnut and made an excuse to leave. Amanda held her head in her hands. 'Something extraordinary has happened, and I don't know if I'm dreaming it.'

Lilly leant forward. 'Go on, you can tell me.'

'Well, after you told me not to shine in secret, I went to the Oracle and had some photographs taken. Now the July edition of the Oracle has been delivered, and I'm not in it. Am I really so old and ugly now that I can't get my photograph in a magazine?'

Lilly tried hard to keep a straight face. 'Oh, I definitely don't think you're old or ugly, Amanda. I think it best that you keep away from the Oracle though. You would be mortified if they said they preferred younger models. Just put it down to experience. It's not wise to keep holding onto your past now that you are about to burst with babies. You can shine as a mother. Yes, that's it. That's when you'll really start to shine.'

Amanda's beautiful face dropped as she fiddled with her wedding ring. 'But what if I prefer my past, Lilly? I'm sure it's a mistake that I've been missed out of the July issue. I should call them.'

Lilly shook her head. 'That's not a wise thing to do, Amanda. Be aware of coming to the wrong conclusion just to suit your own needs – the Oracle will know what they're doing. Just draw a line under your connection with them now to save any embarrassment. That's my advice.'

Amanda sighed and stood up. She pushed her chair back under the table. 'I suppose you're right. I need to keep focused on my charity work. It's the cricket match at the weekend. I'll throw myself into that.'

*

Lilly's heart leapt at the sight of Miles on her doorstep in his cricket whites. 'Well, hello, cousin. You do look handsome, even if I have to say so myself.'

Dressed all in white, with his pale blonde hair, all Lilly could see were his twinkling steel-blue eyes. She felt annoyed with Amanda for not appreciating him. Lilly also felt a bit annoyed with Granny Prue; if she hadn't had an affair with Miles's grandfather, she wouldn't be standing there now with a massive crush on her cousin! Still, the babies were due in six weeks, that would put an end to their friendship – Miles wouldn't have a minute to spare after that.

'Are you coming over to the pavilion to watch the match?'

'Cricket? No, not me, or Melissa either. Melissa's covering for Martyn behind the bar.'

'What are you doing this afternoon, then?'

'Painting. Yes. I'm painting in the shop. Only two weeks now until it opens.'

'I can't believe how quickly that's come around. The time's flown. Well, I'd best be off then. Enjoy your painting.'

Lilly waved Miles off before shouting. 'Make sure you thrash Bertie – it's on your bucket list, remember?'

Miles winked and waved his cricket bat in the air. Lilly closed her front door and with her conscience pricking, headed upstairs to put on her white dungarees. An afternoon in front of the TV was no longer an option. She'd told Miles she was painting, so that's what she needed to do.

*

Seven hours later, a jubilant Miles knocked on the door of Lilly's shop holding a bottle of champagne and two glasses aloft. 'I did it, I thrashed Bertie. Not only that I got this bottle of champagne for being "Player of the Match". I popped in at the pub to have a quick beer and picked up a couple of glasses so that I could celebrate with my cousin.'

'Where's Amanda, can't you celebrate with Amanda?'

'Oh, she's over in the pub with the others. She can't drink in her condition. It's not stopping her having a good time though. She'll still be there at closing time.'

Lilly wiped her hands on her paint-splattered dungarees. 'Well, I suppose a celebratory glass of champagne won't hurt. As you're here, you can help me hang your grandfather's paintings. The walls are dry. Just make sure you watch out for the skirting boards and windowsills. I've only got the front door to paint now, and I can do that tomorrow.'

Miles popped the champagne and handed Lilly a glass. 'Here's to you, Lilly. Two weeks until opening and the shop is looking great.'

Lilly clinked glasses with her cousin. 'Here's to you, Miles. You've crossed an item off your bucket list and won Player of the Match to boot!'

The palest pink walls were the perfect backdrop for

the pomegranate paintings. With a pencil behind his ear Miles focused on drilling the holes for the wall fastenings.

Lilly laughed. 'Has anyone told you that you stick your tongue out when you're concentrating.'

Miles put the drill down and reached for more champagne. 'It's hereditary. My grandfather used to do that. Has anyone told you your violet eyes dance when you laugh?'

'No! But Granny Prue's always did, so I guess that's hereditary too. Do you think our grandparents finally hooked up in heaven?'

Miles placed his glass back on the counter. 'I've never thought about it but, now that you've mentioned it, I'd like to think so.'

'Me too. Granny did mention about not settling for second best.'

Miles checked his watch. 'I'd best get back over the road, Amanda will be wondering where I am.'

Inside the Blue Seagull, Amanda was entertaining a group of young men with stories of her modelling days. Miles placed the empty champagne flutes on the bar and walked over to his wife. 'Come along, Amanda, it's time we went home.'

14

OPENING DAY

The 1st of August had arrived, and Pink Pomegranate Perfumery was due to open at two o'clock. The shelves in the shop were stocked with a full range of products and Mrs Carmichael, as Guest of Honour, sniffed the candles and sprayed perfume with glee. 'Whoever would have guessed my old home could turn into this? Prue would be very proud of you, my dear. Very proud, indeed.'

Lilly had worked non-stop for the last four months to meet today's deadline, and she hadn't had time to think about her achievement. Keeping busy also took her thoughts away from Miles. She was lucky to have had a cousin in her life, albeit for such a short period of time. With the babies due in four weeks, Miles was rushed off his feet doing jobs for Amanda. After they were born, he'd have no time to spare at all.

Melissa tied a pink ribbon across the doorway and handed Mrs Carmichael a pair of scissors. 'I've asked Martyn to take a photograph of you cutting the ribbon at two o'clock, Mrs Carmichael. Lilly can put it on her website.'

Mrs Carmichael checked her hair in the large mirror on the back wall of the shop. 'What a lovely idea, I've always wanted to be famous.'

By one-forty-five a crowd was gathering and, following a wholehearted countdown with ten seconds to go, Mrs Carmichael cut the ribbon to the flash of several cameras. One cameraman was particularly keen. Amanda and Miles stood behind him, and when he caught sight of the former model, he was in his element.

'Amanda, darling! Great to see you. Let's get you into some of the shots. The editor went wild for July's centrefold.'

Melissa placed her hands over her eyes, and Lilly stared at Miles whose face had drained of colour. An Oracle delivery volunteer in the crowd couldn't resist whispering to her friend: 'She was nearly nude, you know. Got a lot of guts, I'll give that to her.'

There was more whispering: 'What edition of the Oracle was it in? I didn't see it.'

Lilly heard the whispers, and she knew that Miles did too. Amanda was in her element. The Oracle hadn't rejected her. She'd just received a dodgy copy of the magazine with the centrefold missing. She felt young and vital again and lapped up the attention of the photographer.

Miles turned around and headed for the pub, followed by Martyn, Ben, and Bertie. Lilly's heart sank, and Melissa's shoulders sagged. Just when things couldn't get any worse, Amanda let out a scream and looked down at her red Jimmy Choo's which were now covered in fluid.

If Lilly didn't like the woman, she despised her now. She wasn't a fit wife for Miles, and she'd ruined the opening of Pink Pomegranate Perfumery by her waters breaking a month early all over Lilly's white sparkle quartz floor tiles.

Mrs Carmichael took control of proceedings. She removed the plastic liner from the bin under the counter and covered the seat of a chair with it. After helping Amanda to sit down, Mrs Carmichael asked Melissa to go to the pub to get Miles. She whispered to Lilly. 'The babies aren't due for a month. Amanda needs to get to the hospital. Miles will know what to do.'

After Miles had driven Amanda away, Lilly cleaned her floor and peered down the promenade to see if there were any customers lingering around to visit her new shop. There weren't. The crowd had well and truly dispersed.

By four o'clock, Mrs Carmichael had eaten several of the canapés, but there were still platefuls left. 'Why don't you shut up shop for today, dear, and take these over to the pub. It's a shame Amanda stole the limelight this afternoon. It will be best to get a fresh start in the morning.'

Lilly agreed. Never had a glass of sauvignon blanc been more needed.

*

It was quiet in the Blue Seagull; Martyn and Melissa were sitting at a table with Ben and Bertie when Lilly walked in with the canapés. Martyn stood up to go behind the bar. 'You look like you need a drink, Lilly. I'll get you a bottle on the house.'

The sea of deflated faces made Lilly's heart sink. 'We nearly did it. We nearly saved Miles from humiliation. What must he be thinking now? His wife betrayed him,' Lilly locked eyes with Martyn as he placed a bottle and a glass on the table, 'by having those photographs taken behind his back. Not only that, but she's also gone into labour a month early with the twin babies he's been longing for.'

Bertie poured the wine for Lilly with shaking hands, and she turned to witness his ashen face. There was silence around the table. Ben's head was bowed, tears welled in Melissa's eyes, and Martyn was now seated, elbows on the table and head in hands. Lilly had a feeling of doom and gloom. 'Will someone tell me what's going on?'

Everyone looked at Bertie, who took a deep breath before speaking. 'Lilly's one of us now, so she needs to know the whole story. Amanda hasn't been the best of wives to Miles. Last Christmas she spiked Martyn's drink and took advantage of him. We've all been worried the babies will have green eyes and messy brown hair. With Amanda and Miles both being blonde with blue eyes, that would look strange.'

Lilly sipped her wine and stared at Martyn through narrowed eyes. 'Well, that's pretty obvious.'

Everyone continued to look at Bertie, who focused his gaze on Lilly. 'I've just had to own up to something, so you need to know as well . . . Amanda accosted me a month before Martyn.'

Lilly raised her eyes to the ceiling. 'Accosted you! I suppose you mean you jumped into bed with her at the first chance.'

Martyn shifted in his chair, and Bertie's cheeks were now aflame. 'OK, I got drunk. Miles was away at a medical conference, and Amanda apparently stayed the night at mine.'

Lilly was livid. 'What do you mean "apparently"?'

'Well, let's just say she made me breakfast in bed. I was shocked. I couldn't remember a thing about the night before.'

Melissa sighed. 'So, we now have another problem. If the babies aren't early, but on time, there's a good chance they'll have black curly hair. That will let Martyn off the hook, but Bertie will need to flee the country. Miles was a boxing champion at school, wasn't he Bertie?'

It was now Lilly's turn to place her head in her hands. 'What a mess. What a total utter mess. I can't bear to look at the two of you.'

Lilly placed her glass on the table and grabbed the bottle before heading home.

*

There was just one more of Granny Prue's envelopes left – the one for August. Miles wouldn't speak to Lilly again when he found out about her collusion with his so-called friends. Lilly needed Granny Prue now more than ever, so she opened the envelope alone.

My darling Lilly,

I knew you would fall in love with Starminster. There's only one thing left on my bucket list now, and that's for you to find the perfect partner. Follow your heart, Lilly – my dreams live on through you.

All my love, Granny Prue xxx

15

A FRESH START

After a disastrous day yesterday, Lilly awoke with renewed enthusiasm. This was the first day of the rest of her life. She could open up her new shop and go to work on a daily basis. Her life finally had structure. Whatever Miles and Amanda got up to was their business. Bertie and Martyn could keep sweating until there was news of the babies, which surely must be sometime today. So, all in all, Lilly was free from all the drama and keen to get on with her life.

There was an internal door from Lilly's cottage to the shop. When she unlocked it at eight-forty-five, she noticed a group of customers gathered outside. Excitement flowed through her veins, and she turned the CLOSED sign on the door to OPEN to let them in.

'How lovely to see you all so early. I do apologise about the official opening yesterday. As a goodwill gesture, all products bought today will be discounted by ten per cent.'

Apart from relocating the business, Lilly had re-vamped the product range. She had kept the best sellers and added three new ranges: Luscious Lavender, Precious Prue, and Lively Lilly.

Mrs Carmichael sniffed them all. 'I love all of these, Lilly. I don't know which ones to choose.'

'Let me help you, Mrs Carmichael: Luscious Lavender is calming, Precious Prue is warm and lingering and Lively Lilly is citrus and fresh.'

'Your grandmother would be so proud of you, my dear. Her memory lives on. I'll take one of everything in the Precious Prue range for now. Is there a hint of gardenia in it? I always remember Prue using gardenia soap.'

'So do I, Mrs Carmichael and, yes, the top note is gardenia.'

'Clever girl. You're a real expert in this field. Well done you!'

Lilly held her shoulders back and sniffed the mismatch of aromas being squirted throughout the shop. Bertie had been so kind with allowing her to use his barn indefinitely. Lilly much preferred creating and producing her own products than shipping them in bulk from China. It was Lilly's ambition that once all the old stock had gone, her shop would be full of her authentic creations. Pink Pomegranate Perfumery was taking on a whole new life, just like its owner.

Mrs Craddock stood admiring the pomegranate watercolour paintings. 'These are Harold Herriot's, aren't they? My mother was friends with his wife, Henrietta – or Hetty as she was best known. I used to play in the garden of their cottage when I was a young girl. I'll always remember Harold's pomegranates.'

Lilly was struck that she didn't know Miles's grandfather's first name. 'Oh, yes they are, Mrs Craddock. Miles has loaned them to me. It was a bit of a coincidence that my perfumery is named after pomegranates.'

Lilly wrapped two Luscious Lavender candles and a room spray in Pink Pomegranate tissue paper for Mrs Craddock and tied the package with a silver ribbon. 'There you go, Mrs Craddock. Thank you so much for popping in today. I'll be over to the tea room for another slice of your amazing lemon drizzle cake before too long.'

Flora, from the fish and chip shop, handed Lilly a basket full of products to wrap. 'We've needed a shop like this in the village for ages, Lilly. I'm sure you'll do a good trade. My son, Oscar, is due home soon. I'll send him around to see if he can help you out.'

Lilly frowned, she knew that Flora and Alfie had just celebrated their tenth wedding anniversary. 'Oscar? Are you sending him around after school?'

Flora laughed heartily. 'Oscar's from my first marriage. He's thirty-five now. I know I look good for my age, but I'm well past having little ones still at home.'

Lilly blushed. 'Oh, I see. How can Oscar help me out?'

'Oscar is a buyer for Nouveau Heritage. He's based in London. They're always on the lookout for original products, things that are a bit different. You won't be going far wrong if you win his approval. As I say, he'll be home soon. He's planning on taking a long weekend in September so that he can come to visit us. He's such a busy boy.'

Lilly reached for a white carrier bag with new "Pink Pomegranate Perfumery" logo and carefully placed the tissue wrapped products inside for Flora. 'Here you go. Thank you so much for popping in today. I'd love to meet Oscar when he comes home. Have a good day!'

By one o'clock, the morning's customers had dispersed, and Lilly placed her GONE FOR LUNCH sign in the window. She felt a huge sense of satisfaction. Such a luxury as closing for lunch wouldn't be allowed in London or any cities or towns she could think of. However, in a seaside village such as Starminster, it seemed precisely the right thing to do. Lilly was starting to love life. A sandwich and soft drink in the Blue Seagull were calling; Lilly wanted to update Melissa on her successful morning.

Melissa was busy behind the bar. 'Lilly! Have you had any news yet from Miles?'

Lilly shook her head. With all the excitement of this morning, she'd managed to put the thought of Amanda delivering babies out of her mind.

Melissa's eyes darted to the pub door when it opened and then back to Lilly. 'Martyn and Bertie have gone into town out of the way in case it's bad news and Miles turns up to skin one of them alive. What do you think he'll do if it's obvious one of his best friends has fathered the twins? I'm at my wit's end.'

Lilly didn't need this. Amanda had spoiled yesterday, there was no way she was going to ruin today too. Lilly required at least one day's rest from that atrocious woman.

'I have no idea of what's going to happen, Melissa, and I don't care. Can we change the subject? I'd like a tuna and cucumber sandwich please and a Diet Coke. Did you know that Flora has a thirty-five-year-old son who works for Nouveau Heritage?'

Melissa poured the Diet Coke. 'You're right, Lilly. I need to stop panicking. There's nothing we can do at the moment, so let's not talk about it. I'm sorry I didn't ask about your first morning in the shop. How did it go? And, yes, I'm well aware of Oscar – I used to go out with him.'

Lilly's eyes lit up. 'Really? You need to tell me all the sordid details before he comes home next month. Is he dishy? Do you think I'll be able to charm him into buying my products for Nouveau Heritage?'

Melissa smiled. Lilly was good for her. If the baby thing all went wrong and Martyn was responsible, then Melissa would need Lilly more than ever.

*

An hour for lunch just wasn't long enough. Lilly was laughing as she left the pub and crossed the road to Moonbeam Mews to be met by Miles sitting on the wall outside.

'Miles! Why didn't you come into the pub? Don't answer that. Is Amanda OK? Has she had the babies?'

Miles sat with shoulders slumped and tears in his eyes. 'Can I come into yours, Lilly?'

Lilly unlocked the door to her cottage, and Miles followed her in before sitting on the sofa, head in hands. 'The babies aren't mine, Lilly.'

Lilly sat down next to Miles. 'What makes you say that, Miles?'

'They are two perfect little boys with full heads of black hair.'

Lilly visualised slapping Bertie across his already inflamed face. 'Black curly hair doesn't necessarily mean they're not yours, Miles, does it?'

'Not black curly hair, black straight hair. The babies are half-Chinese, Lilly. They can't be mine.'

Lilly gulped, and her head thumped. Mr Ling! Amanda talked about all the times he looked after her in China Town in London.

'Oh, I see. What are you going to do?'

'I've left her. It was only the babies that were keeping us together. She'll be in the hospital for a few days, and I've told her she needs to find alternative accommodation when she comes out. I'm going home now to pack up her things and put them in storage to collect when she's ready. She's lucky I'm prepared to do that. Amanda won't be coming back to Starminster, or Little-Bee-Lost Cottage ever again.'

Lilly felt a tremendous sense of relief, not for Martyn or Bertie, but for Miles. 'Let me come and help you. I'll close the shop this afternoon. If we do it together, we'll get through it in no time. It feels awful now, but before long you will realise this has all happened for the best. I'm sure of that, Miles, I really am.'

16

NEWS TRAVELS FAST

The gate to Little-Bee-Lost Cottage creaked as it was pushed open, causing Reverend Hartley to peer over the wall of the churchyard. 'Good afternoon, Miles, and to you, Lilly. Any news of the newest members of our community yet?'

Miles held the gate open for Lilly to walk through to the garden of the cottage, then turned around and walked towards the rose-covered gateway of St Mary's Church. Reverend Hartley strode over the cobblestones to join him.

Miles held his shoulders back. 'What I am about to tell you, will shortly spread like wildfire around the village. I am wise enough to know that it will eventually become yesterday's news and my life will, for once, take on some normality. But, for now, I need space and time to process the fact that Amanda cheated on me and I have left her.'

The Reverend held onto a crumbling wall. 'Oh, my goodness, Miles. Has Amanda given birth yet?

'Yes, and the babies aren't mine, Reverend. They so obviously aren't mine. When Amanda leaves the hospital, she will be taking the babies elsewhere, they will not be coming back to Starminster.'

Reverend Hartley felt a sense of relief. Amanda had caused a lot of troubled souls in the village. The confessions he'd heard from the least likely members of the parish had disturbed him greatly.

Miles waited for an onslaught of goodness and reasoning as to why he was doing the wrong thing. It didn't come.

'Well, I am very appreciative of the update, Miles. Mrs Craddock and the wonderful village volunteers will be arriving shortly to decorate St Mary's for the flower festival. I am sure questions will be asked.' The Reverend raised his eyebrows and stared at Miles.

Miles forced a smile. 'Well, that will be a good opportunity for you to pass on my news. The sooner it's out in the open, the sooner my nightmare will be over.'

Reverend Hartley nodded and brushed his dusty

hands on his jeans. 'I really must get this wall fixed; it's weathered far too many storms. We all need a bit of help when we've weathered a storm. I'm pleased to see you have the support of Lilly in your moment of crisis. I can assure you, Miles, that you will be in the hearts and minds of all our parishioners too.'

Miles felt a weight lifting. He had approval from the nearest thing to God. How could confessing to the Reverend that he had left Amanda high and dry with two babies to look after be accepted without question? Miles frowned and headed back to the cottage where Lilly was sitting on a bench outside the front door.

'I've done it, Lilly. I've opened up a whole can of worms that will keep the predators of Starminster well-fed for months.'

Lilly smiled. 'Well done, cousin. Now let's go inside and have a clear out. I take it the rice cakes can go?'

Miles smiled warmly. 'I don't know what I'd do without you, Lilly. Thanks for coming to my rescue.'

*

It was four o'clock before news of Amanda's infidelity reached the Blue Seagull. Melissa became nauseous when a thirsty flower arranger divulged the news over a glass of lemonade. 'So, you see, he's left her. The babies aren't his. Good for Miles, that's what I say.'

Melissa sent a text to Martyn:

NOT GOOD NEWS. MILES HAS LEFT HER.
BABIES NOT HIS.

Martyn's heart sank, and he showed the text to Bertie whose blood pressure went through the roof. 'What do we do now? Do we go back to face the music? Tell me, Martyn, what should we do?!'

'I think we should stay away until things have calmed down. We can say we went on a road trip and your car broke down.'

'My Ferrari? No-one will believe that!'

Bertie's phone vibrated with a text from Lilly:

YOU'RE BOTH OFF THE HOOK. COME
HOME NOW. I'M WITH MILES.

Bertie showed the text to Martyn whose green eyes glistened with relief before his phone rang with a call from Melissa.

'Lilly just called. Miles asked her to. The babies are half-Chinese – can you believe it?! Miles has left Amanda, and she won't be coming back to Starminster again. Lilly needs you to pick up the storage boxes from Bertie's barn and help them out at Little-Bee-Lost Cottage. All traces of Amanda need to be removed by tonight. I'm arranging cover at the pub, so I can help too. You and Bertie are the luckiest men alive. We need to focus all our energy on Miles now to help him through this.'

As they packed Amanda's clothes into cases and black plastic sacks, Lilly's curiosity kept the conversation flowing.

'You must tell me all about your grandparents, Miles. Apart from the fact that your grandfather and my grandmother had a fling and that your grandfather loved pomegranates, I know nothing about them. I realised that yesterday when Mrs Craddock said they were called Harold and Henrietta.'

Miles forced himself to reminisce; he knew what Lilly was doing. She was trying to take his mind off the present by thinking back to the past.

'It was a strange situation, now that I think back to it. I was very close to my grandfather, he was either in the garden tending to his vegetable plot and his greenhouse full of pomegranates, or he was in the conservatory painting. One thing I can say, though, is that he always had time for me. On the other hand, my grandmother was rarely at home. She belonged to several committees, and they took up the majority of her time.'

'Where were your parents, Miles, when you were growing up? You haven't mentioned them at all.'

'In New York.'

'In New York! What on earth were they doing over there? Why didn't they take you with them?'

'My father is a world-renowned scientist, and my mother, a former model who relishes dressing up for award ceremonies and dinner parties. I didn't fit into their lifestyle. It was my grandfather who suggested I remain in Starminster and live a "normal" life. My parents jumped at the chance to offload me.'

Lilly stood with mouth agape and watched as Miles calmly walked over to the window before smiling. 'The cavalry has arrived, armed with packing boxes. I don't know what I'd do without my friends. Thanks for rallying everyone around, Lilly. Let's get rid of this unfortunate part of my life so that I can finally get on track to normality. I owe that to my grandfather.'

Lilly couldn't resist a question. 'What's "normal", Miles?'

Miles looked over his shoulder on his way out of the room. 'I don't know yet, Lilly. But I aim to find out.'

17

NEW OPPORTUNITIES

September had arrived and brought with it the homecoming of Oscar. Flora burst into Lilly's shop with her arm linked through her son's. 'Lilly, this is Oscar, my little boy!'

All six-foot-four-inches of Oscar stood before Lilly with his arm outstretched. Lilly took hold of his tanned hand and felt a firm, confident handshake. Oscar was wearing a navy suit and open-necked white shirt, his aftershave was warm and spicy, and Lilly could just imagine this black-haired, blue-eyed gorgeous man, roaming the floors of the shop in which he worked. Yes, Oscar, was very much a "Nouveau Heritage man".

Lilly was dumbstruck as Oscar's twinkling eyes roamed her face, taking in her violet eyes and long brown hair, which she twisted around her forefinger as her cheeks flushed. 'Hi, Lilly. I'm very pleased to meet you. Mother has told me all about Pink Pomegranate Perfumery. She speaks highly of your products. I've checked out your website and wouldn't mind a browse around your shop if that's satisfactory to you?'

Lilly nodded. 'Of course, please feel free … make yourself at home … do anything you like … I can provide a box of samples if that would help … just let me know if you need anything.'

Flora's smile lit up the room as she whispered. 'I knew you'd charm him round, Lilly. I can tell he likes you. He needs a reason to come home more often – you could be it.'

Oscar sprayed the perfumes onto tester strips and surveyed all the products on offer before giving his opinion: 'Clever name, the mention of "Pomegranate" balances out the risk of too much femininity. The watercolour paintings are great as they give the shop a feel of authenticity. I suggest you launch a unisex range. I can see you attracting men into this shop.'

Oscar placed an arm around his mother and headed for the door. Flora stopped in her tracks. 'Is that it then, Oscar? Don't you need to invite Lilly out to dinner to discuss her business further?' Flora elbowed her son in his ribs and whispered, 'Don't be so rude.'

A smiling Oscar turned around. 'I haven't been in

the Blue Seagull for a while. Will you join me for dinner at seven-thirty, Lilly?'

Lilly wiped her clammy hands on her dress. 'Oh, yes, of course, that would be nice. I'll see you at seven-thirty.'

The shop door closed, and Lilly sat down behind the counter to stop her knees from knocking. She couldn't stop her heart from thumping though – as far as she was concerned, she had received approval from Nouveau Heritage. They may not want to stock her products yet, but Oscar had been impressed. He'd even recommended she expand her product range. He liked the "authenticity" and said he could see men wanting to come to her shop. Lilly was ecstatic.

*

By seven-thirty, Lilly had her new product range mapped out. She'd changed into a short cream dress, piled her hair high on her head and wore a pair of amethyst earrings. Lilly was ready to do business.

Martyn's tropical green eyes popped when Lilly glided into the pub. 'Wow! Look at you. Hot date?'

Lilly smiled. 'Business meeting. Is Oscar here yet?'

The door to the pub opened, and Oscar walked in. He saw Lilly standing at the bar and went over to join her. 'Hi Martyn, long time no see. I'm having dinner with this gorgeous lady tonight. A nice quiet table in the restaurant for two please.'

Martyn led the way into the restaurant and handed menus to Lilly and Oscar. Lilly's eyes sparkled. 'I'm so glad you like my shop, Oscar. I appreciate your thoughts, and I have come up with an idea for a unisex range. I am going to call it: Never-Bee-Lost.'

Oscar raised an eyebrow and Lilly continued, 'All my new ranges must mean something. I've so far developed: Luscious Lavender (after my family name); Precious Prue (after my grandmother); and Lively Lilly (after me).'

Oscar leant on the table and stared into Lilly's eyes. 'You'll have to enlighten me as to why I would choose a fragrance from your collection called "Never-Bee-Lost". I just don't get it.'

Lilly beamed. 'Oh, you will get it, Oscar, when you hear the story. There was once a lost little bee in the garden of the man who grew pomegranates and painted the watercolours in my shop. He named his cottage: Little-Bee-Lost. It's here in Starminster on the hill next to the church – you must have heard of it. Anyway, I want to turn the story into something positive.'

Oscar was intrigued. 'Go on, explain in more detail.'

'Well, in my unisex Never-Bee-Lost range, there will

be three fragrances: Forever Belong, Normality and Moonbeam Encounter.'

Oscar reached for his glass of champagne which Martyn had just poured from a chilled bottle now sitting in a floor-standing ice bucket next to the table. 'You're an amazing woman, Lilly. I think you may be onto a winner there. Where does "Moonbeam" come into it?'

Lilly reached for her glass too. 'Oh, that's another story. You can trust me that everything's authentic, though.'

Oscar clinked glasses with Lilly. 'We'll talk business again when your new range is developed. For now, you can tell me all about you, and why such an attractive woman has found her way to Starminster.'

Martyn had made sure the table for two in the restaurant could be seen from the bar. He stood behind it with Melissa. Bertie sat on a barstool and turned around to watch Lilly's dinner date unfold. 'I would never have guessed that Oscar was Lilly's type.'

Melissa scowled. 'Neither would I.'

Bertie felt her annoyance. 'There's nothing still going on between you two, is there? I heard he got that job at Nouveau Heritage and just upped and left without so much as a thought for those he left behind. I remember Flora being heartbroken at the time.'

Melissa blushed and lowered her eyes. Bertie decided not to challenge her further, and Martyn couldn't take his eyes off Lilly. She looked fantastic tonight; how come he hadn't noticed before. With all the worry about Amanda, he'd put women out of his mind. Maybe it was time to make a move on Lilly. As far as Oscar was concerned, he shouldn't be allowed anywhere near Lilly, not after he broke Melissa's heart. No, Oscar wasn't going to get things all his own way this time – Martyn would never let that happen again.

18

DOUBLE DATE

On Saturday morning, Oscar sat in Mrs Craddock's Tea Room enjoying toasted teacakes with his mother when the door opened, and Melissa breezed in. 'Morning, Mrs Craddock! My usual fresh cream doughnut to take away please.'

Oscar's conscience pricked. He hadn't finished things well with Melissa when he upped and left for London. He regretted that. He was also perturbed that he still had feelings for her. Melissa turned around and headed towards the door. Oscar caught hold of her arm as she passed his table.

'Melissa! Will you have dinner with me tonight? I'm only here for the weekend.'

Melissa pulled her arm free. 'You've got a nerve. Lilly last night – me tonight.' Melissa bent down and stared into Oscar's deep blue eyes before quietly spurting out the words: 'It'll probably be Mrs Craddock on Sunday night, then you'll be off to London again.'

Flora cringed. She'd always liked Melissa – she was embarrassed that Oscar had mistreated her. She remembered the day the poor girl found out Oscar had deserted her and run off to London. Melissa had stormed into the fish and chip shop and left her engagement ring on the counter. Flora still had it in her jewellery box.

With eyes locked, Melissa noticed tears welling in Oscar's. Was he in pain? Did he have a heart after all? He'd indeed lost his arrogant exterior. 'Please, Melissa. We can go into town to the Bistro. We need to talk.'

Melissa threw her shoulders back, her heart pounding. 'Pick me up at seven.'

The door to the tea room slammed, and Flora looked at her son. 'You still love her, don't you, Oscar? Maybe now your career has taken off you can pick things up where you left off with Melissa. She's never had another boyfriend. Maybe there's still a chance.'

Martyn was annoyed when Melissa broke the news of her date. He rushed over the road to the Pink Pomegranate Perfumery and begged Lilly to go to the

Bistro with him that evening. He explained they needed to keep an eye on Oscar and Lilly was keen to be there in support of Melissa. Engaged!? Oscar and Melissa had been engaged!? Suddenly, going into business with a man who had treated her friend so badly didn't seem appealing at all.

*

Lilly met Martyn in the pub just before seven. They sat at a table and waited for Oscar to arrive to collect Melissa. He arrived with a minute to spare, and Melissa's light footsteps could be heard running down the stairs behind the bar. Oscar rushed to greet her with a kiss on the cheek and Martyn strode forward, followed by Lilly. 'Any chance of a lift into town? I'm taking Lilly to the Bistro.'

Melissa narrowed her eyes and stared at her brother. Oscar was taken aback. 'We're going to the Bistro; I've booked a table for two for seven-thirty.'

Martyn smiled through gritted teeth. 'What a coincidence, so have I. We'd best get going then. Is that your BMW outside? They're not very roomy in the back, are they? I'd best sit in the front with my long legs.'

Lilly suppressed a giggle before whispering to Melissa. 'I wish I had a brother like Martyn to protect me. He's only doing this out of the kindness of his heart, and he's roped me in as a decoy.'

On arrival in town, Oscar rushed inside the Bistro ahead of the others. 'I have a table for two booked. Can you make sure it's a private table, as far away as possible from other tables for two?' He handed the waiter a twenty-pound-note and turned around to open the door for the others to enter.

Martyn wasn't able to hear the discussion at his sister's table, but he could see a twinkle in Oscar's eyes. Did Melissa just touch his hand? What was she doing playing with her hair? Lilly sensed Martyn's anxiety. 'There's not a lot we can do for the next couple of hours. It's a real nuisance we're stuck at the far end of the room. Oscar's not exactly going to get down on one knee and propose again, is he? It'll just be an innocent catch up to talk about old times.'

Martyn dragged his gaze from Oscar to Lilly, and his heart softened. She looked amazing in that turquoise dress. Her brown hair was piled high again, accentuating her pretty face, and she had a way with her that made him relax.

'Now, Martyn, which wine would you recommend to go with the sea bass? I'm not having a starter as I've seen the dessert menu, which will leave me spoilt for choice!'

Oscar reached for Melissa's hand. 'I've been such a

cad. I put work before you, and I've always regretted it.'

Melissa's heart leapt. 'But you love your job, Oscar. You wouldn't be able to move back to sleepy Starminster after living in London.'

Oscar pressed Melissa's fingers to his lips. 'You're right, but there's nothing to stop you from moving to London with me. We can take up where we left off. I have an apartment with amazing views of Tower Bridge. I can just imagine us there now having dinner overlooking the Thames. Take a leap of faith, Melissa, come back with me when I leave on Monday.'

*

In the bar at the Blue Seagull, it was surprisingly quiet. Martyn and Melissa both off on a Saturday night was unheard of. Bertie questioned the temporary staff who would only say that they had gone on a double date to the Bistro in town with Oscar and Lilly.

Bertie relayed the news to Ben who was enjoying a pint in Little-Bee-Lost Cottage with Miles. 'That was Bertie on the phone. He's "Billy no mates" tonight in the pub and wants us to join him.'

Miles hadn't been in the pub for the last six weeks. Apart from going to work, he hadn't been anywhere.

Ben stood up. 'The gossip's died down now, Miles.

Trust me. You have to start socialising again. The sooner you do it, you'll feel a whole lot better. Two pints of Starminster are calling us, and I'm not taking "no" for an answer.'

*

Martyn had an irresistible urge to kiss Lilly. He stared at her mouth as she chatted away about her time in Tillingtree and her holidays in Starminster when she was younger. She even told him about her ideas for a unisex range in the perfumery.

Lilly loved Martyn's stories about his time growing up with Ben, Bertie and Miles and laughed heartily at the many pranks they got up to. 'You should write a book, Martyn, just like Granny Prue. Her book looks hilarious. I've not had time to read it all yet, but I aim to. I've just been so busy getting the perfumery off the ground.'

Melissa looked over her shoulder as Oscar guided her out of the Bistro with his hand on the small of her back. She was pleased that Martyn and Lilly were having a good time. Sitting in the front seat of his BMW, Melissa leant over to kiss Oscar. 'Do you really think we can make this work?'

Oscar held Melissa's face in his hands. 'I have no doubt.'

It was nine-thirty before Martyn noticed his sister

and her ex-fiancé had disappeared. He asked the waiter to order a taxi.

At ten o'clock, Lilly and Martyn were back in the pub to be greeted by Ben, Bertie, and Miles. Lilly was delighted to see them, especially Miles, who had finally resurfaced. She rushed over to their table and sat down. Martyn joined them. 'You'll never guess what! Martyn took me to the Bistro in town so that we could spy on Melissa and Oscar and they did a runner. Have they turned up here yet?'

The men shook their heads, and Bertie raised his eyebrows. 'Don't tell me those two are getting back together.'

Ben downed his pint and walked up to the bar to buy a round of drinks. There was no way Melissa would be getting back with Oscar – not if he had anything to do with it.

19

CHOICES TO MAKE

The following morning, Ben burst into the perfumery. 'I need your help, Lilly. Martyn called me to say that Melissa's planning on moving to London with Oscar. We can't let it happen. We just can't.'

Lilly noticed Ben's eyes glistening, and she opened the adjoining door to her cottage. 'Take a seat on the sofa. I'll lock the shop up for a bit so you can tell me all about it.'

Ben wrung his hands together. 'I know she would never fall for me, but I love her, Lilly.'

There was a knock on the window of the shop. Lilly jumped up to see Miles peering inside. 'Stay there, Ben. I'll just see what Miles wants; I'll be back soon.'

Lilly shut the adjoining door and unlocked the shop for Miles to enter. He handed her a bunch of pale pink roses. 'Freshly picked this morning from the cottage garden. I thought they'd look good in your shop.'

Lilly was shocked at the sudden transformation of Miles; she had been worried that he was becoming a recluse. 'They're lovely, Miles. Thank you. It was great to see you in the pub last night.' Lilly lowered her voice. 'Have I got my cousin back?'

Miles grinned as he blushed. 'Maybe.'

Lilly was conscious of the heartbroken Ben on her sofa. 'I really must pop next door; there's something I need to sort out. Thank you so much for popping in. We must meet up soon for a catch-up.'

Miles headed for the door. 'I've finished reading your grandmother's book. What do you think about the chapter entitled "Melon Man"?'

Lilly snorted and threw a hand to her mouth. 'I haven't read that chapter yet. I will do, though, just as soon as I get time.'

Miles smiled and waved as he walked back down the promenade. Martyn turned around and headed back to the pub. He threw the bunch of flowers he'd bought in the general store that morning into a bin. So, Doctor Miles had eyes for Lilly. There was no way he could compete with that.

Lilly placed an arm around Ben's shoulders. 'I often wondered if anything was going on between you two. I can sense the chemistry. You took Melissa to the Bistro once, didn't you? Didn't that go well?'

'It went really well. I know when I'm beaten, though. Why would Melissa want a village solicitor when she can have any man she wants? I won't let that buffoon break her heart twice though – I'm determined to put a stop to that.'

Lilly sighed. 'I'm so annoyed with you, Ben. I'm annoyed with me too. I should have tried to get you two connected. You're perfect for each other. I've just been lost in my own world. I'm no better than Oscar, putting my business first. Don't worry; all is not lost. There must be a way to turn this around.'

Sundays were never busy in the shop, so Lilly asked Bertie around for a coffee. 'Can you keep a secret, Bertie?'

Bertie grinned. 'Always.'

'Well, we need to get Oscar off the scene so that Ben can hook up with Melissa. Do you have any suggestions?'

Bertie scratched his chin. 'I like a quandary. Those two have been dancing around one another for years. I've often wondered why Ben can't find the courage to tell her how he feels. If it helps, I could lend him my

Ferrari for a day. They could go on a drive and take a picnic. That would work.'

Lilly raised her hands in the air. 'But we need to get rid of Oscar. He's about to take Melissa to London. How do we make her see sense?'

Bertie closed his eyes for a few seconds. 'It's a shame Amanda's not around. We could have sent her off in Oscar's direction. He's not above temptation; I can tell you that.'

Lilly pulled at her hair. 'Why are there so few young women in Starminster?!'

Bertie reached for his phone. 'Leave it with me. I have some favours I can call in. I sold some new apartments in the next village recently to some very eligible ladies. All over me they were to get to the top of the list. That apartment block is on a prime development site; sea view, indoor/outdoor pools, gym, the works.'

Lilly narrowed her eyes. 'Do whatever you need to. But you'd better do it quick! Oscar needs to show his true colours before tomorrow, at all costs!'

*

By two-thirty, Oscar was being driven to the new apartment complex by Bertie in his yellow Ferrari. 'Trust me, Oscar. The ladies who have bought these apartments are rich. You'll find Nouveau Heritage products galore in their walk-in wardrobes. Just give them your business cards and promise to have dinner with them when they're next in London. When they're let loose in your shop, they'll spend thousands. View it as a bit of customer service you're doing on your weekend off – spreading the word in these remote parts to the rich and famous.'

'Famous? Are they famous?'

'Err … undoubtedly. I can't go into detail, though. Confidentiality Act and all that.'

*

Ben couldn't wait for Lilly to sort out his problem. He needed to do it himself. He walked into the Blue Seagull and, with Melissa behind the bar, took his destiny into his own hands. 'I love you, Melissa, and I hope that one day you can grow to love me too. I want us to grow old together here in Starminster. Don't go back to that loser. Stay here with me.'

Melissa's knees buckled, and Ben walked behind the bar to embrace her. 'Will you stay with me, Melissa? I promise we can make this work.'

Melissa nodded, and Ben swept her up into his arms. 'We need to celebrate. Martyn can cover for you this afternoon. You're coming home with me.'

*

At five o'clock, Lilly received a call from Bertie. 'His head wouldn't turn. It just wouldn't turn! Mine certainly would have, but old Oscar only has eyes for Melissa. What are we going to do?'

Bertie could sense Lilly's smile down the phone. 'There's nothing to worry about. Martyn called. Melissa's going nowhere. She's in love with Ben, not Oscar. Ben sorted it out all by himself.'

Bertie punched the air. 'Yesss!!! I'll meet you in the pub for a pint to celebrate. What a team. We did it!'

Lilly phoned Miles. 'You need to come down to the pub. We've got some great news. No, I won't tell you over the phone. Come to the pub!'

20

MELON MAN

With all the excitement of the last few weeks, things were starting to calm down for Lilly. Melissa and Ben were loved up. Miles had reintegrated himself into the group of friends, and Bertie wasn't short of admirers from the ladies in the apartment complex. He had taken Martyn over there a couple of times, and Lilly was pleased about that. Martyn had gone back to his usual withdrawn self after their dinner at the Bistro in town, Lilly hoped he would find love soon like his sister.

Anyway, tonight was a free night, and Lilly settled down on her sofa to finish reading Granny Prue's book. It was November, and there was a noticeable chill in the air. Lilly wrapped a fleece blanket around her shoulders and slipped her feet into her UGG slippers. A glass of sherry was the appropriate tipple for tonight – Granny Prue was always partial to sherry. Lilly plumped up the cushion behind her and began to read:

> *And then there was Melon Man … He grew them in his greenhouse … He took photographs of them too … Iris rode her bicycle down the hill to visit him … His wife was rarely at home … Iris filled the gap … But then it all went wrong … The day Melon Man planned to run away with Iris, his wife told him she was carrying a baby … She did not tell him that baby was not his … Iris gave birth to Melon Man's child, and he became the father to another man's son …*

Lilly read the chapter again and again and picked out all the salient points. They were buried in there amongst Granny Prue's natural wit and wisdom, but to her – and surely to Miles – they stood out like fireflies in a sandstorm. Granny Prue was writing about herself and her one true love; she'd changed pomegranates to melons, paintings to photographs and uphill to downhill to put her readers off the scent of her secret. Also, people who knew her were aware that she had never ridden a bicycle in her life – she thought they were horrendous contraptions.

Lilly was astounded by her grandmother's

ingenious creativity. Only two people would guess she was writing about herself: her granddaughter and her doctor – the ones who knew her middle name. Prudance Iris Lavender was crafty beyond belief.

Harold Herriot was Lilly's grandfather; he wasn't related to Miles. Therefore, Lilly and Miles weren't cousins. Granny Prue had followed her own advice: Keep secrets safe until they can be told.

Lilly felt embarrassed, awkward, shocked. Trust Granny Prue to reach out from beyond the grave. Lilly sent a text to Miles:

I'VE JUST READ MELON MAN.

Half an hour later, Lilly opened her front door to the sight of Miles. 'Is it acceptable for someone who's not your cousin to come in at this time of night?'

Lilly poured Miles a sherry. 'I'm in total and utter shock. Your grandmother was a conniving woman! She tricked your grandfather – sorry my grandfather – into believing she was having his baby, which led to my grandmother leading a sorrowful, broken-hearted life.'

Miles smiled. 'I still view him as my grandfather – Harold Herriot was the best thing that ever happened to me. I don't think Prue lived a sad life either. She had your father, and you.'

'But she didn't walk down the aisle at St Mary's

church to the Wedding March! Your grandmother put a stop to that by lying to your … my grandfather. Just think how differently things would have turned out if your grandmother had been honest.'

'Well, let's think about that. If my grandmother had been honest, we wouldn't both be sitting here now. OK, Harold would have probably got together with Prue, but Hetty would have been shipped off somewhere with her baby. My father wouldn't have grown up in Starminster and neither would I. You and I would never have met, and that would have been such a shame.'

'Why would it have been a shame?'

'Because I've had a crush on you since you were six. You don't appear to remember me, but I remember you. You used to run up the hill to St Mary's church when you came for your summer holidays. When you saw me, you waved. Your father was never far behind. You collected stones that fell from the walls of the churchyard. What did you do with those stones?'

Lilly's eyes widened, and she chuckled. 'I built a wall in the garden of our London house. Only a small wall for my dolls to peer over. Those stones reminded me of Granny Prue's and our visits to Starminster. I used to count down the days when I knew we were coming back on holiday again. Why didn't you speak to me?'

'Oh, I was very shy when I was ten. I'm not shy now, though.'

Lilly blushed. 'Would you like a clotted cream biscuit to go with that sherry?'

'That would be great! Thanks, Lilly. By the way, did you open the last envelope from your grandmother back in August, or are you waiting for us to do that together? I'm sorry I've been like a bear with a sore head for months.'

Lilly blushed again. 'It's not a problem. I opened it.'

'What did it say?'

'That there was just one thing left on Granny Prue's bucket list – she wants me to find the perfect partner.'

Miles opened the packet of biscuits before staring at Lilly. 'Maybe I can help with that.'

Lilly lowered her eyes and poured herself another sherry in an attempt to look busy. She daren't look at Miles. Was he flirting with her? She thought he was her cousin just a few hours ago. She needed time to process this dramatic change. 'Do you think the villagers have worked out about the affair between Harold and Granny Prue?'

'Have any of them ignored you in the street, or tried to trip you up?'

'No.'

'Me neither. I think we're safe then. Prue was such a great writer I had to read that chapter four times to establish what she was trying to say between the lines. She'll be thrilled her secret's out now, though. How ironic that my grandparents were in a loveless marriage, just like Amanda and me. Hetty and Amanda cheated on the both of us. My grandfather never knew and had to soldier on, but my case is out in the open, and I have the chance to change my life.'

Lilly's stomach somersaulted as realisation hit her. 'I want you to have a happy life, Miles.'

Miles leant forward to kiss her. 'Your wish is granted. I can guarantee we'll both have happy lives from this moment on.'

21

CHINESE WHISPERS

Christmas at Lorne House had taken on a whole new meaning. Bertie wandered around the grounds and relished the excitement the Christmas market had brought to his childhood home. When his family had relocated to their Scottish residence two years ago, Bertie had remained behind with his Estate Agent business. However, he hadn't anticipated how lonely he would become; the seaside house now felt quite empty.

Everything changed though after Lilly arrived in Starminster. Apart from the Christmas market being her suggestion, she had advertised for help with her growing business, and several new faces to the community had emerged in the barn at Lorne House. Over the last few weeks, Bertie made sure he introduced himself to everyone assisting Lilly bottle and package her new unisex product range. Lilly had also developed a Christmas range which Mrs Carmichael was taking great pleasure in selling at one of the market stalls. Mrs Craddock was one of her customers.

'I'll take four of the Spicy Spruce reed diffusers, please. Any news of how things are going between Miles and Lilly?'

Mrs Carmichael tightened her red shawl against the icy wind and straightened her lace cap before answering. 'Fingers crossed; it's all going very well.'

'Didn't waste much time, did they? Amanda was here one minute, gone the next. Lilly was ready and waiting. Mind you, after what Miles has been through, that relationship has my approval.'

Mrs Carmichael pulled her shawl even tighter as Mrs Craddock continued, 'I always felt sorry for Prue with the father of her baby deserting her. Hetty Herriot knew all the details; my mother was fascinated by the stories she told. Now, if Hetty had written a book, it would have been a darned sight juicier than Prue's comedy of errors.'

Mrs Carmichael raised her eyebrows. 'What did Hetty say about the father of Prue's baby?'

'He was a hippie in the swinging sixties – only in Starminster for the weekend. He swept Prue off her feet after a couple of pints of Starminster Ale. She paid a pretty heavy price for a one-night stand.'

'Shocking! Poor Prue. I always had the impression that the father of Prue's baby was the love of her life, not a hippie. Still, that was Prue for you – always looking through rose-coloured spectacles. I loved her book, though. I'm a bit younger than her and couldn't picture all the colourful characters she wrote about. I'm sure she embellished a lot of the stories; Prue had a great imagination.'

Mrs Craddock huffed. 'My mother always kept me up to date on everyone in the village. It took me a while to work out who Melon Man was though.'

'Who was he?'

'Old Hanratty who lived on his allotment with his wife. Like chalk and cheese those two, she was quite well-to-do. He built a fence around it with a gate and even made a greenhouse out of old window frames – it was a monstrosity. The residents fought to have them evicted for years.'

'Oh, dear! I wonder who Iris was then?'

'She'll have been staying at the campsite on top of the hill. She was up a hill somewhere – the story says she rode her bike down it to meet Melon Man. The campsite was an eyesore too, thank goodness it was closed down years ago. They both got their comeuppance in the end. Hanratty brought up a child that wasn't his, and Iris had to flee in shame.'

Miles clung to Lilly behind Mrs Carmichael's stall. 'I've heard of Chinese whispers, but this level of inaccurately transmitted gossip just breaks the mould.'

Lilly giggled. 'If those two haven't worked out Granny Prue's secret from the grave, then her reputation will remain forever intact. A drunken hippie is much more palatable than a major love affair with a local married man.'

'*I'm* still a married man.'

'That doesn't count. You'll be free soon enough.'

Lilly leant her head on Miles's shoulder. 'It's a shame Nouveau Heritage has turned my products down. But not a surprise.'

Miles stroked her hair. 'You don't need them; you're doing amazingly well on your own. I have to say I'm pleased Oscar's out of the picture for Melissa's sake. Martyn and Ben would be falling over themselves to punch him if he ever put a foot wrong again. I'd punch him too if he came near you.'

Bertie coughed. 'Come along, young lovers. I need your thoughts on whether I should take Sophie, Bridget, or Amy to the carol service at St Mary's tonight. I'm spoilt for choice. Best thing I ever did letting Lilly use my barn, my love life's picked up no end! I've gone from zero to hero if you know what I mean. Still, it always helps when the ladies see the family estate in conjunction with my dashing good looks.'

Miles laughed. 'Let's go and choose a date for Bertie then. With Lilly's help, romance is blossoming in Starminster. Even Martyn's got a girlfriend.'

Bertie's head spun around. 'Who? What have I missed? I've been far too busy helping Lilly get the Christmas market off the ground to go to the pub.'

Lilly grinned. 'Now that would be telling. You'll have to find out for yourself. I introduced Martyn to online dating. It didn't work for me, but it seems to have worked wonders for him.'

In the barn, Ben and Melissa supervised the temporary staff. Melissa's eyes shone as she looked at Ben. 'It's amazing how much things have changed since Lilly moved to Starminster. Prue would have been delighted with the buzz going on in the village. I still can't believe it's because of the perfumery that we finally got it together. Now there's a thought – *Pink Pomegranate Perfumery: The perfect remedy for romance.* Lilly should use that slogan on her website.'

Ben visualised Oscar's not so smug face when Melissa told him to take a hike. 'Who needs the help of

Nouveau Heritage? Lilly's going global on her own.'

The helpers in the barn stood with mouths open, and Amy gasped. 'Did you hear what she just said? I'm going to have a squirt of this one. I'll have a man by the end of the day. I need a remedy for romance.'

Sophie made a mental note to let all her friends know that Pink Pomegranate Perfumery had turned down a deal with Nouveau Heritage – the business was going global on its own. It was always good to get a bit of inside information; the price of the products would shoot up soon – best to buy now.

Bridget raised her eyes and carried on bottling fragrances in silence. Sophie and Amy were so gullible – there was no remedy for romance. Bridget should know, she hadn't had a date in over twelve months.

Two minutes later, Bertie bounded into the barn and stood in front of Bridget. 'I, err, I just wondered if you would accompany me to tonight's carol service at St Mary's church. It's just a thought.'

Miles and Lilly peered around the barn door catching the attention of Ben and Melissa. Miles winked and put his thumb up. Melissa suppressed a giggle. Sophie and Amy waited for Bridget's answer, and Bertie was turning a bright shade of pink. Bridget nodded, and Ben punched the air. Sophie whispered to Amy, 'Just wait until everyone hears about this!'

22

THE CAROL SERVICE

The village volunteers had excelled themselves with the Christmas flower arrangements. They had even decorated the large Nativity stable. Reverend Hartley turned a blind eye to the silk daffodils and tulips standing proudly next to the crib. He knew they had been recycled from Easter, and that cost was of the essence.

Lilly and Miles sat at the back of the church, saving two seats for Melissa and Ben. With only sixty-four seats, they couldn't save places for everyone. It didn't matter, Bertie didn't see them as he walked down the aisle towards the front with Bridget on his arm. Melissa and Ben arrived, followed soon after by Martyn and his new girlfriend – they sat behind Bertie and Bridget.

With the church full and several villagers standing at the back, the organist began to play a hearty rendition of *Hark the Herald Angels Sing.* This was followed by *Away in a Manger* which led to Reverend Hartley's annual Christmas address. Mrs Carmichael could conduct the sermon herself if ever needed. She knew all the words; nothing much changed in Starminster.

Ding Dong Merrily on High soon reverberated around the inner sanctum of God's Holy place, and when it ended, there was a change to proceedings. Reverend Hartley stood at the pulpit and put on his reading glasses.

Mrs Craddock nudged her friend. 'I knew he needed glasses. That's the first time he's worn them. I'm sure he guesses all those bible readings or makes them up as he goes along. Quite clever if he does.'

There was silence amongst the congregation, and the Reverend spoke: 'That was Prudance Lavender's favourite Christmas carol, it will always remind me of her. I was fortunate enough to spend an afternoon with Prudance two weeks before her untimely passing. She wanted to tick another item off her bucket list and asked me to join her for a helicopter ride. If you've never had the pleasure of flying in a helicopter then I can assure you, it's the most exhilarating experience.'

There were giggles from the congregation.

Reverend Hartley continued, 'On that joyous

occasion, while we were circling high in the sky above St Mary's, Prudance shared with me the most remarkable story. Nearly sixty years ago, just two days before Christmas, Prudance gave birth to her baby son in the back pew of this very church.'

There were gasps and heads spun around to witness the scene of the birth. Bertie was stunned to see the woman sitting behind him. 'Rachel!' There was a sea of "shushes" and Bertie turned back to face the pulpit.

'You may wonder how Prudance managed; it would have been a terrifying time for her, all alone in a darkened church. I asked her this question, and Prudance responded by saying it was a "Christmas miracle". Through her excruciating pain and blurred vision, she saw a light. A light bobbing around in the churchyard. A light that grew stronger and stronger until it was shining upon her.'

The congregation was entranced, and Reverend Hartley looked up from his notes. 'God was watching down on Prudance, and he intervened in her hour of need. It was a rare occasion when Dr Harold Herriot entered God's house, but he entered that night to help Prudance. He could give no explanation as to why he was drawn to the church in the middle of the night to safely deliver a bouncing baby boy.'

Miles winked at Lilly, and she whispered in his ear,

'I didn't know your grandfather was a Doctor?'

Miles whispered back, 'I don't think it was a miracle, your grandmother would have tipped him off.'

Reverend Hartley folded his notes and smiled at the congregation. 'The miracle didn't end there. Two days later Dr Herriot's wife gave birth to a baby boy on no other than Christmas Day! A remarkable story, don't you think? A shining example of divine intervention in its purest form. Now for our last carol of the evening: *Silent Night.*'

With the carol service over, the congregation began to spill outside into the churchyard. Rachel linked arms with Bertie. 'Hello, brother! Are you surprised to see me? I've come down from Scotland to spend Christmas with you at Lorne House.' Rachel gazed up at Martyn who was standing next to her. 'Meet my new boyfriend!'

Bertie's mouth fell open, and Bridget stood awkwardly behind him. 'You're going out with Martyn!'

'I certainly am. I've fancied him for years.'

Martyn blushed. 'We met online. Lilly suggested I tried it.'

Miles went over to thank Reverend Hartley for his uplifting service and to ask him a question. 'When my divorce from Amanda comes through, I want to marry Lilly. Would we be able to have a blessing in the church so that Lilly can walk down the aisle to the Wedding March?'

Reverend Hartley raised his eyebrows. 'Does Lilly know about this?'

Miles shuffled his feet. 'Not yet. I thought I should check with you first.'

'Well, I'm very honoured to be privy to your intentions. Prudance will be delighted that Lilly has found the perfect partner. It would give me great pleasure to conduct a blessing of your union at St Mary's.'

Lilly stood next to Bridget; the poor girl had been deserted by Bertie now that his favourite sister was back on the scene. 'Shall we head back down the hill to the pub? We can get ahead of the rush.'

Bridget screwed her nose up. 'Pubs aren't my scene – it's obvious that Bertie and I aren't suited. Between you and me, I can't stand the colour of his car. It was embarrassing when he picked me up in it earlier. Who would buy a yellow Ferrari? I'm going to head off home; he won't notice.'

Miles placed an arm around Lilly as Bridget headed off. 'We should have chosen Sophie; she's more Bertie's type.'

Lilly smiled up at Miles. 'I think we should leave things well alone. Bertie will sort himself out eventually. He'll be thrilled that Rachel's back. All he needs is a bit of company. Can you remember her from before? Would you have thought she was a match for Martyn? Online dating never worked for me.'

'I used to go out with her.'

Lilly punched Miles on his shoulder. 'You used to go out with her!'

'I was fourteen at the time and bought her an ice-cream in the park one Sunday afternoon. I bought her a soft drink the following week when we went for a walk on the beach. Our relationship fizzled out after that. There was a girl I much preferred, but she only came down to Starminster once a year for her holidays, and she never spoke to me. All I got was the occasional wave.'

Lilly was distracted, a weed had grown on Granny Prue's grave, she had to pull it out before it took over and ruined the neatly tended plot. Miles followed her as she strode over to the white marble headstone before stopping in her tracks. A blue flower stood tall in the centre of the holly and mistletoe wreath Lilly had laid on her grandmother's grave that morning.

Lilly gulped. 'It's an iris. I haven't planted any irises. Irises don't bloom until May.'

Miles turned Lilly around to look at him. 'It's another of your grandmother's miracles. She must have heard me speaking to Reverend Hartley and is excited that you will get to walk down the aisle at St Mary's to the Wedding March.'

'What?? I'm not getting married, am I?'

Miles knelt on one knee and produced a solitaire diamond ring. 'Will you marry me, Lilly Lavender? Just as soon as I'm divorced – I don't want to wait a day longer than that. Reverend Hartley will give us his blessing.'

Lilly nodded and burst into tears. Miles pushed the ring on her finger and kissed her.

Bertie turned around to see what Melissa and Ben were looking at. Ben nudged Martyn. 'We need to take bets on who's going to be Best Man. I think it could be me, as Miles trusted me with his secret. I had to plant that silk iris on Prue's grave before I went into church tonight. Melissa managed to get hold of it – we can't believe how lifelike silk flowers are these days. Much better than those old daffodils and tulips in the Nativity stable.'

Reverend Hartley gave the organist a thank you gift before she left the church that evening – a potted poinsettia. He much preferred real flowers to silk. He sighed; he really must put his foot down next year with the flower arrangers. Those daffodils and tulips were an eyesore.

On his way out of the church, the Reverend looked up at the starlit navy sky, and his thoughts turned to Prudance Lavender. He walked over to her grave to admire the pink and white cyclamen Lilly had planted last week. As soon as he saw the iris, his heart pounded. Another Christmas miracle!

Reverend Hartley looked to the sky before speaking: 'There can't be anything left on your bucket list now, Prudance dear. Lilly is going to carry out your cherished dream of walking down the aisle at St Mary's to the Wedding March. I need to ask for your forgiveness; I was so enthralled with the story you told me when we last met that I forgot to thank you for the helicopter ride. Thank you, Prudance,' the Reverend held a hand to his pounding heart, 'and thank you for bringing miracles to Starminster.'

EPILOGUE

Five Years Later

'Mummy, Daddy! They're growing! If I sit here, I can watch them growing!'

Miles joined his three-year-old son on the sunny patio at Little-Bee-Lost Cottage. The hardy potted pomegranate tree, a wedding present four years ago from Bertie, had for the first year begun to bear fruit. 'You're right, Harry, they are growing. We will have to wait a few weeks yet though before we can pick them.'

'Are Ben and Missa coming today?'

'Yes, Ben and Melissa are coming for lunch, along with Martyn, Rachel and Bertie.'

'Why?'

'Because they all want to have fun with you and to meet your sister.'

Lilly joined the boys on the patio. 'She's having a sleep. That's good timing; I can finish preparing the food before everyone arrives. Would you like to help me, Harry? We need to fill the cake we made this morning with jam and cream.'

Harry jumped up and down in delight and Miles grinned at his wife before mowing the lawn.

Rachel was the first guest to arrive, armed with pink helium balloons. Lilly threw her arms around her. Rachel had become integrated into their group of friends since her arrival at the carol service five years ago. Her "no strings attached" relationship with Martyn suited them both and Bertie was delighted to have his sister back at Lorne House.

Rachel now worked for Lilly, and with the help of her marketing skills, Pink Pomegranate Perfumery was producing products to sell globally. Granny Prue's cottage in Moonbeam Mews had become the Head Office for six staff, and Rachel was Lilly's deputy. It had been a godsend having someone to keep an eye on the business while Lilly was on maternity leave.

Rachel whispered to Lilly. 'You'll never guess what – Nouveau Heritage finally want to stock our products.'

Lilly raised her eyebrows. 'I couldn't do that to Melissa. I don't want Oscar visiting us for meetings and stirring things up between her and Ben. They're getting married in two weeks. I can't risk that.'

Rachel smiled. 'Oscar now works in Amsterdam. He left Nouveau Heritage at the end of last year. That must be why they've contacted us now. I've no doubt he's been standing in our way. A bit spiteful, don't you think?'

Lilly clapped her hands. 'Invite them down to Starminster for a meeting. If they're keen, they'll jump at the chance. I'll sort out a childminder for the day. I've got lots of offers of help from the villagers and the staff in the barn at Lorne House, are you sure you and Bertie are OK with me still using it?'

'I've told you before, Lilly. Your staff in the barn are more than welcome. Bertie's in his element with all the comings and goings. I just wish I'd come back to Starminster sooner; Martyn tells me Bertie was spending most of his time in the pub before I came home.'

Ben and Melissa arrived with Martyn, followed by Bertie in an orange Porsche. Harry ran to the gate to greet Bertie. He loved the noisy orange car.

A whirring noise from the sky grew louder until it became quite deafening. Harry shouted: 'Copter, Copter!!'

The bright blue helicopter circled St Mary's church before landing in a field next to it. Reverend Hartley bent down as he climbed out and ran under the circling blades. He noticed the group gathered at the fence of Little-Bee-Lost Cottage and walked over to speak to them.

'Good afternoon, everyone! I have just had the most exhilarating experience. It's my seventieth birthday today, and the village volunteers treated me to a helicopter ride. You could say it's been on my bucket list to have another go in one. Prudance certainly taught me a thing or two about living life to the full.'

There were cheers, and congratulatory words for the Reverend and Bertie offered to take him for a thrill-seeking ride in his Porsche whenever he wanted. Reverend Hartley smiled and changed the subject:

'You've most likely been too busy over the last week with the birth of baby Iris, but I cast an eye over Prudance's grave most days. Lilly always does such a good job with it; I like to see the flowers blooming. Fresh flowers are always my preference. Anyway, I don't know how you did it, Lilly, but those pink irises started blooming on Wednesday and have made an amazing display. In all my years I've never seen irises that colour before. Anyway, I must be off now, enjoy your afternoon.'

Lilly narrowed her eyes at Ben and Melissa. 'You've done it again, haven't you? You planted silk flowers on Granny Prue's grave as soon as you knew I'd given birth to a girl! Reverend Hartley will be holding this up as another Starminster miracle. You do realise that, don't you?'

Ben and Melissa shook their heads and held their hands in the air. Lilly stared at Miles, and Bertie made a decision. 'We need to find out what's been going on. Let's take a trip over to see Prue.'

Standing around Prue's grave, the friends were astounded. The pink irises were real, not fake. Bertie whispered to Rachel, 'I've heard of "pushing up daisies", but Prue's surpassed herself to do this!'

Miles bent down beside the white marble headstone with baby Iris in his arms. 'You had an amazing great-grandmother, Iris, one day we'll tell you all about her. Your mother called her Granny Prue.'

Harry skipped around the grave. 'Ganny Poo! Ganny Poo!!'

The helicopter whirred into life, and everyone watched it rise into the sky, creating a bluster throughout the churchyard. Bertie turned to Martyn. 'Did Reverend Hartley want a ride in my Porsche or not?'

Martyn laughed. 'Don't think so. I said you should have bought a black one.'

The group of friends headed back to Little-Bee-Lost Cottage, with Miles carrying Iris and Bertie holding onto Harry's hand. Lilly turned around before walking through the rose-covered gateway to take in the sea of pink on Granny Prue's grave. It may not be a miracle, but it was certainly a sign. Prudance Iris Lavender was happy with the way things had turned out for her granddaughter. Lilly looked to the sky and hoped with all her heart that things were going just as well for Granny Prue – wherever she may be.

****

Printed in Great Britain
by Amazon

24837800R00091